CONTEMPORARY AMERICAN FICTION

PLAN B FOR THE MIDDLE CLASS

Ron Carlson's fiction has appeared in *The New Yorker,* *Harper's, Playboy, Gentlemen's Quarterly, Ploughshares, Story,* and many other journals. His work has been widely anthologized and his monologues performed in a dozen cities. He lives with his family in Tempe, Arizona, where he directs the Creative Writing Program at Arizona State University.

PLAN B

FOR THE

MIDDLE

CLASS

STORIES

RON CARLSON

PENGUIN BOOKS

PENGUIN BOOKS
Published by the Penguin Group
Penguin Books USA Inc., 375 Hudson Street,
New York, New York 10014, U.S.A.
Penguin Books Ltd, 27 Wrights Lane, London W8 5TZ, England
Penguin Books Australia Ltd, Ringwood, Victoria, Australia
Penguin Books Canada Ltd, 10 Alcorn Avenue,
Toronto, Ontario, Canada M4V 3B2
Penguin Books (N.Z.) Ltd, 182–190 Wairau Road,
Auckland 10, New Zealand

Penguin Books Ltd, Registered Offices: Harmondsworth,
Middlesex, England

First published in the United States of America by
W. W. Norton & Company, Inc., 1992
Reprinted by arrangement with W. W. Norton & Company, Inc.
Published in Penguin Books 1993

1 3 5 7 9 10 8 6 4 2

PUBLISHER'S NOTE
These are works of fiction. Names, characters, places, and incidents
either are the product of the author's imagination or are used
fictitiously, and any resemblance to actual persons, living or
dead, events, or locales is entirely coincidental.

THE LIBRARY OF CONGRESS HAS CATALOGUED THE HARDCOVER
AS FOLLOWS:
Carlson, Ron.
Plan B for the middle class: stories/Ron Carlson.
p. cm.
ISBN 0-393-03370-8 (hc.)
ISBN 0 14 02.3117 X (pbk.)
I. Title.
PS3553.A733P57 1992
813´.54—dc20   91–42257

Printed in the United States of America
Set in Baskerville
Designed by Margaret Wagner

FOR ELAINE

CONTENTS

CONTENTS

III

ACKNOWLEDGMENTS

The stories in this collection first appeared, sometimes in slightly different form, in the following publications:

Gentlemen's Quarterly, "DeRay," "Sunny Billy Day"

Harper's, "The Summer of Vintage Clothing"

McCall's, "A Kind of Flying"

The New Virginia Review, "Plan B for the Middle Class" (as "Plan B")

The New Yorker, "On the U.S.S. Fortitude"

Playboy, "Hartwell"

Ploughshares, "Blazo"

The Santa Monica Review, "Fort Bragg"

Story, "The Tablecloth of Turin"

Weber Studies, "The Golf Center at Ten-Acres"

"A Kind of Flying" also appeared in *The Wedding Cake in the Middle of the Road,* edited by Susan Stamberg and George Garrett.

"On the U.S.S. Fortitude" was anthologized in *Voices Louder than Words, A Second Collection,* edited by William Share; and in *The Practical English Handbook,* Ninth Edition, edited by Watkins and Dillingham.

Thanks also to the Sundance Institute for a week with "Blazo."

I

HARTWELL

This is about Hartwell, who is nothing like me. I have sometimes told stories about people, men and sometimes a woman, who were like me, weak or strong in some way that I am or they shared my taste for classical music or fine coffee, but Hartwell was not like me in any way. I'm just going to tell his story, a story about a man I knew, a man not like me, just some *other* man.

Hartwell just didn't get it. For years he existed, as the saying goes, *out of it.* Let's say he wasn't alert to nuance, and then let's go ahead and say he wasn't alert to blatancy either. He was alert to the Victorian poets and all of *their* nuances, but he couldn't tell you if it was raining. This went way back to when he was in college at the University of Michigan and everybody was preparing for law school taking just enough history, political science, things like that, but Hartwell majored in English, narrowing that to the Victorians, which could lead only to one thing: graduate school. As a graduate student, he was a sweet guy with a spiral tuft of light hair that rose off his head like fire, who lived alone in a room he took off campus and who read his books, diligently and with pleasure, and ate a steady diet of the kind of food eaten with ease while reading, primarily candy.

When I met him, he had become a sweet, round man, an associate professor of English, who taught Browning and Tennyson, etc., etc., and who brought to our campus that fall years ago his wife, Melissa, a handsome woman with broad shoulders and shiny dark hair cut in a pixie shell.

I say "our campus" because I too teach, but Hartwell and I couldn't be more different in that regard. I know what's going on around me. I teach rhetoric and I parse my students as well as any paragraph. My antennae are out. I can smell an ironic smirk in the back row, detect an unprepared student in the first five minutes of class, feel from the way the students file out of class what they think of me. Hartwell drifts into his classroom, nose in a book, shirt misbuttoned, and reads and lectures until well after the bell has rung and half the students have departed. He doesn't know their names or how many there are. He can't hear them making fun of him when they do it to his face while handing in a late paper, whining his name into five sarcastic syllables, *Pro-fess-or Hart-well,* and smiling a smile so fake and sugary as to make any of us avert our eyes. He is oblivious.

This was apparent to me the first time I met him with Melissa at the faculty party that fall. The effect of seeing them standing together in the dean's backyard was shocking. Anyone could see it: they wouldn't last the year. As I said, she was attractive, but as she scanned her husband's colleagues that evening it was her eyes, her predatory eyes, that made it clear. Poor old Hartwell stood beside her, his hair afloat, his smile benign and vacant, an expression he'd learned from years alone with books.

Melissa shopped around for a while, and by midterm she was seeing our Twentieth-Century Drama professor, a young guy who had a red mustache and played hand-ball. It took Hartwell the entire year to find out about the affair and then all of summer session to decide what it meant. Even then, even after he'd talked to Melissa and she to him and *he'd* moved out of the little house they were buying near the college, even then he didn't really wake up. The students were more sarcastic to him now that he was a cuckold, a word they learn as sophomores and then overuse for a year. Watching that was hard on me, those sunny young faces filing into his office with their million excuses for not being present or prepared, saying things that if I heard them in my office would win them an audience with the dean. Things I wouldn't take.

I, however, am not like Hartwell. There isn't a callow hair on my head. I am alert. I am perspicacious. I can see what is going on. I've become, as you sense, a cynical and thoroughly jaded professor of rhetoric. My defenses are up and like it or not, they are not coming down.

It was in the period just after Melissa that I became friends with Professor Hartwell. Our schedules were sim-ilar and many afternoons at four-thirty we fell into step as we left the ancient Normal Building where we both taught. Old Normal was over a hundred years old, the kind of school building you don't see anymore: a red block structure with crumbling turrets, high ceilings, and a warped wooden floor that rippled underfoot. I'd walk out with Hartwell and ask him if he'd like to get a coffee. The first time I asked him, he said *what* and when I had repeated the question, he looked at me full of wonder, as if I'd invented French roast, and said, "Why, yes, that sounds like a good idea." But, of course, with Hartwell that was the way he responded every time I asked him. He was like a child, a man without a history. His experience with Melissa certainly hadn't hurt him. He thought it was odd, but as he said one day, over two wonderful cups of Celebes Kolossi at the Pantry, about the drama teacher, "He had vigor." But we primarily talked shop: semantics. Hartwell was doing a study of Gerard Manley Hopkins, and I offered my advice.

I wasn't surprised during this time to see him occasionally lunching with Melissa. He was the kind of man you could betray, divorce, and then still maneuver into buying you lunch.

But our afternoons together began to show me his loneliness. He was as seemingly indifferent to that feeling as any man I'd ever met, even myself in the life I have chosen, but more and more frequently during our conversations I would see his eyes narrow and fall upon a table across the room where a boy and a girl chatted over their notebooks. And when his eyes returned to me, they would be different, and he would stand and gather his books and go off, a fat fair-haired professor tasting grief. He never remembered to pay for his coffee.

Then the next thing happened, and I knew from the very beginning what to make of it. When you fall in love with a student, three things happen. One: you become an inspired teacher, spending hours and hours going over every tragic shred of your students' sour deadwood compositions as if holding in your hands magic parchment, suddenly tapping into hidden reservoirs of energy and vocabulary and lyric combinations for your lectures, refusing to sit down in class. Two: the lucky victim of your infatuation receives a mark twice as high as he or she deserves. Three: you have a moment of catharsis during the denouement in which you see yourself too clearly the fool, a realization that is probably good for any teacher, because it will temper you, seal your cynicism and jade your eye, and make you sit down once hard and frequently thereafter.

The object of Hartwell's affections was a girl I kind of knew. She had been in my class the year before, and she was a girl you noticed. Ours is a small midwestern college and there are a dozen such beauties, coeds with the perfect unblemished faces of pretty girls and the long legs and round hips of women. These young creatures wear plaid skirts and sweaters and keep their streaming hair in silver clips. They sit in the second row and have bright teeth. They look at you unseeing, the way they've looked at teachers all their lives, and when one of these girls changes that glance and seems to be appraising, you wear a clean shirt and comb your hair the next day.

That was what gave Hartwell away: his hair. I met him on the steps of Normal and he looked funny, different. It was the way people look who have shaved beards or taken glasses, that is, I couldn't tell what was different for a moment. He simply looked *shorter*. Then I saw the comb tracks in the hair plastered to his head and I knew. He had been precise about it, I'll give him that. After a lifetime of letting his hair jet like flame, wildfire really, he had cut a part an engineer would have been proud of and then formed the perfect furrows across the top of his head and down, curling once to disappear behind the ear. If you'd just met him, I suppose, it didn't look too bad. But to me, god, he looked like the concierge for a sad hotel. He had combed his hair and I knew.

There were other signs too, his pressed shirt, the new tie, his loafers so shiny—after years of grime—that they hurt the eye. He was animated at coffee, tapping the cover of the old maroon anthology of Victorian poetry with new vigor, and then the *coup de grâce*—one afternoon at the Pantry, he picked up the check.

Hartwell was teaching a Hopkins-Swinburne seminar at night that term and the girl who was the object of his affections, a girl named Laurie, was in that evening seminar. When Hartwell began to change his ways, I simply noticed it. It was none of my business. One's colleagues do many things that one doesn't fully appreciate or understand. But Hartwell was different. I felt I should help him. He had not been around this particular block, and I decided to stay alert.

I could see, read, and decipher the writing on the wall. This shrewd pretty schoolgirl was merely manipulating her professor to her advantage. I knew she was an ordinary student from her days in rhetoric, an officer in Tri-Delta sorority who wore a red kilt and a white sweater and who spent more time choosing her blouses than studying verb phrases, and now she was out for poor Hartwell.

I changed my office hours so I could be around when his class broke up, which was about nine P.M. Tuesday and Thursdays, and I saw her hang around my old friend, chatting him up, always the last to leave and then stroll with him, and that is the correct word, *stroll*, down the rickety corridor of Normal, the floor creaking like the fools' chorus. She would laugh at the things he said and toss her hair just so and squeeze her books to her chest. And Hartwell, well, he would beam. From the door of my office I could see the light beam off his forehead, he was that far gone.

In most cases these things are not really very important, some passing infatuation, some shrewd undergraduate angles to raise his or her grade point average, some professor's flagging ego takes a little ride, but I watched that term as it went further and further for Hartwell. The shined shoes were a bit much, but then at midterm that spring, he showed up one day in gray flannel slacks, his old khakis and their constellations of vague grease stains gone forever. And I could tell he was losing weight, the way men do when they spend the energy necessary to become fools.

Melissa, his ex-wife, now uneasily married to our drama professor (who had since developed his own air of frumpiness), came to my office one day and asked me what was going on with Hartwell. I hadn't like her from the beginning, and now as she sat smartly on the edge of the chair, her short carapace of hair as shiny as plastic, I liked her even less, and I did what I am certainly capable of doing when required: I lied. I told her that I noticed no difference in her former husband, no change at all.

I knew with certainty that there was danger when one afternoon in April he leaned forward over his coffee and withdrew a sheet of type paper from the pages of his textbook. It was a horrid thing to see, the perfect stanzas typed in the galloping pica of his office Underwood, five rhyming quatrains underneath the title "To Laurie." It was fire, it was flower, it was—despite the rigid iambic pentameter—*unrestrained*. It was confession, apology, and seduction in one. I clenched my mouth to keep from trembling while I read it, and after an appropriate minute I passed it back to him. He was eager there at the table in the Pantry, beaming again. He had begun to beam everywhere. He wanted to know what I thought.

"It is very, very good," I told him quietly. "The metaphors are apt and original, and the whole has a genuine energy." Here I leaned toward his bright face. "But Hartwell. Don't you ever, under any circumstances, give this to a student."

"I knew it was good," he said to me. "I knew it. Do you see? I'm writing again."

"Do not," I repeated, "give this to Laurie. You will create a misunderstanding."

"There is no misunderstanding," he told me, folding the poem back into the old maroon book. "It is a verity," he said. "I am in love."

As everyone knows, there is nothing to say to that. I stirred my coffee and saw from how high an altitude my friend was going to fall.

April is a terrible month on a campus. This too is a verity. Every pathway reeks of love newly found and soon to be lost. It is one of the few times and places you can actually see people *pine*. The weather changes and the ridiculous lilacs bloom at every turning, their odor spiraling up the cornices of every old brick building in sight, including, of course, Old Normal. Couples lean against things and talk so earnestly it makes you tired. Everywhere you look there is some lost lad in shirtsleeves gesturing like William Jennings Bryan before a coed, her dreamy stare a caricature of importance. This goes on round the clock in April, the penultimate month in the ancient agrarian model of the school year, and as I walked across campus that spring, I kept my eyes straight ahead. I didn't want to see it, any of it.

Of course, Hartwell and I couldn't be more different. That's clear. But I had a sensation after he'd left that afternoon that reminded me too strongly of when I had my troubles, such as they were. Years ago, a lifetime if you want, a student of mine became important to me. She wasn't like Hartwell's Laurie—at all—her name isn't important, but it wasn't a pretty name and—in fact—she wasn't really a pretty girl, just a girl. She came to my notice because of an affliction she carried in her eyes, a weight, a sorrow.

This is not about her anyway, but about me in a sordid way. I saw what I wanted to see. What I needed to see. She was frail and damaged somehow and I was her teacher. Well, who needs details? It was the same story as all these other shallow memories, some professor off balance and a young person either willingly or unwillingly the victim or beneficiary of it all. My student, this strange girl, received an A for B work, and I waited for her to pick up her term paper a week after the semester ended. Let me explain this to you: there was no reason for me to be on campus, sitting in my office in Normal Hall, no reason whatsoever. I had my door cracked one inch and I waited. Tuesday, Wednesday, Thursday, Friday. On Friday afternoon I was still on the edge of my chair. Just having her paper (which I read and reread, held in my lap as I waited) was enough, and undoubtedly, it would have powered me through the weekend. I am the kind of professor who is in his office more Saturdays and Sundays than he will ever admit. On Friday evening, when I was preparing in my routine way to leave and go home, she came. I heard a step on the stair, the first step which was not the janitor's step, and I knew she was coming. How long could it have taken between the sound of those beautiful footsteps and their pausing at my opened office door? Twenty seconds? Ten? Whatever the time, it was the eon between my young and my old selves. I had a chance, as the old scholars put it, to know my tragic flaw. Not that I'm any more than pathetic, and certainly not tragic, but I came to know in that short moment that I was a fool and that I was about to join a legion and august company of the history of all fools. The girl came to my door and paused and then knocked on the open door. She acted surprised to find me there. She acted as if she expected to retrieve her paper in a box outside my door. I told her no, that I had it. I handed it to her, still warm from my lap. She nodded and averted her eyes and said something I'll never forget. "This was a good class for me," she said. "You made it interesting." And then she turned and touched the rippled floor of Normal Hall for the last time. Without her paper and with no reason to be on earth on Friday night, I became a fool, and in a sense the guardian of fools.

Like Hartwell.

But what could I do? This Laurie was as shrewd as any I'd seen come along. She not only accepted his poem—she'd commented on it. I'd quizzed him on what she had said, but he'd just smiled until his eyes closed, and shook his head. He was so far gone that I had to smile.

But Laurie hadn't stopped there. With no reason whatsoever, she had invited him to the Spring Carnival. There was no reason to do this. She'd already won her victory. Hartwell was absolutely incandescent about it. He was carnival this and carnival that. I should come, he said. Oh go with *us*, he said. It was as if they were engaged. I told him no. It was a sunny spring afternoon in the Pantry, too hot really to be drinking coffee, and I told him no to go ahead, but for god sakes be careful. If you want to know the meaning of effete, just say *be careful* to a fool in love. My advice didn't get across the table.

The Spring Carnival on our campus is a bacchanalian festival. It is designed with clear vengeance: victory over winter has been achieved and this celebration is to make sure. Years ago, it was held on the quad and consisted of a few quaint booths, but it has grown, exploded really, to the point where now every corner of campus is covered with striped tents and the smell of barbecued this and that clouds the air. I haven't been in years.

But. Hartwell's invitation was tantalizing, and then it was all tripled by something that happened the last week of classes. I was packing my briefcase in my office in Normal when the door opened. There wasn't a knock or a hello, the door just swung open and Hartwell's Laurie was hanging on it, half out of breath, her blond hair swinging like something primeval. "Oh, good," she said. "You're here. Listen, Downey," she said, using my nickname without hesitation, "Hart and I are going to the carnival and he mentioned you might like to go. Please do. You know it's Friday. We're going to eat and then take it all in." Hartwell's Laurie looked at me and smiled, her tan cheeks not twenty-two years old. "It's going to be fun, you know," she said and closed the door.

Well, an interview such as that makes me sit down, and down I did sit. I took the old old bottle of brandy out of my bottom drawer, a bottle so old my father had bought it in Havana on one of his trips, and I had half an ounce right there. Downey. I was jangled. So she and Hartwell called me Downey, when they called me anything. The prospect of being talked about set part of me adrift.

To the carnival I went.

But I didn't go with them. I told Hartwell that I might see him at the carnival, but to go ahead. It was the last week of classes and I had a lot to read. Friday afternoon I was plowing through a stack of rhetoric papers when— outside my window—I heard the Gypsy Parade, the kazoos and tambourines that signal the commencement of festivities. A feeling came to me that I hadn't had in years. I had heard this ragtag music every spring of every year I'd been in Normal Hall, but this year it was different. It called to me. I felt my heart begin to drum, and I put down my pen like a schoolboy called outside by his mates. It was the last Friday of the school year and I was going to the carnival.

Part of all this, naturally, was a sympathetic feeling I had for Hartwell. Laurie had invited him to the carnival, after all. I was—and I'll admit this freely—happy for him. At the corner I stopped and bought a pink carnation and pinned it to my old brown jacket and I thrust my hands into the pockets and plunged into the carnival. The crowds of shouting and laughing merrymakers passed around me in the alleyway of tented amusements. It was just sunset and the shadows of things ran to the edge of the world, giving the campus I knew so well an unfamiliar face, and I had the sense of being in a strange new village as I walked along. Bells rang, whistles blew, and a red ball bounced past. I saw Melissa, Hartwell's former wife, on the arm of one of our Ph.D. students, eating cotton candy. By the time I'd walked to an intersection of these exotic lanes, I had two balloons in my hand and it was full dark.

I bought some popcorn and walked on beneath the colored lights. Groups of students passed by in twos and threes. They didn't see me, but I know that I had taught some of them. I felt a tug at my arm then and it was Laurie, saying, "Downey. Great balloons!" She had Hartwell by the other arm.

"Yes," I said, smiling at both of them and tugging at the two huge balloons. "They're big, aren't they?"

Hartwell was in his prime. He looked like a film actor and confidence came off him in waves. He wore a new white flannel jacket and a red silk tie. "They're absolutely grand!" Hartwell said. "They're the best balloons in this country!"

Laurie pulled us over to a booth where for a dollar a person could throw three baseballs at a wall of china plates. The booth was being managed by a boy I recognized from this semester's rhetoric class, though he wouldn't make eye contact with me.

"I want you two to win me a snake," Laurie said, pointing to the large stuffed animals that hung above our heads.

"Absolutely," Hartwell said, reaching in his pocket for the money. Hartwell was going to pitch baseballs at the plates. It was a thrilling notion—and when he broke one with his final throw, that was thrilling too.

"Well," I said. "If we're going to ruin china, I'm going to be involved." I paid the boy a dollar and threw three baseballs, smashing one plate only.

We stayed there awhile, acting this way, until on my third set, I broke three plates, and the boy, looking as shocked as I did, handed me a huge cloth snake. It was pink. Hartwell was right there, patting my back and squeezing my arm in congratulation, and I imagine we made quite a scene, Laurie kissing my cheek and smiling as I handed her the prize. I'll say this now: it was a funny feeling there in the green and yellow lights of the carnival—I'd never been patted on the back before in my life. I am not the kind of person who gets patted on the back, which is fine with me, but when Hartwell did it there, calling out "Amazing! Magnificent!" it felt good.

We floated down the midway, arm in arm after that, until I realized we had walked all the way down to Front Street, which is the way I walk for home. I said good night to them there, Hartwell and I bowing ridiculously and then shaking hands and smiling and Laurie kissing my cheek lightly one more time and calling, "Good night, Downey!" I turned onto Front Street and then turned back and watched them walk away, Laurie tightly on Hartwell's arm. They stopped once and I saw them kiss. She put her hand on his cheek and kissed his lips.

As I moved down Front Street, the noises of the carnival receded with every step and soon there was just me and my two balloons in an old town I knew quite well.

It is not like me to enter houses uninvited. I have never done it. But I was in a state. I can't describe the way I felt walking home, but it was about happiness for Hartwell and a feeling I had about Hartwell's Laurie. I had begun to whistle a lurid popular tune that I'd heard at the carnival. This should tell you something, because I do not whistle. And when I came to Old Tilden Lane, where all the sorority houses are lined up, I turned down.

I'd been to all of the Greek houses at one time or another. Each fall, the shiny new officers invite some of the faculty out to chat or lecture or have tea in the houses, and we do it when we're younger because it counts as "service" toward tenure or we're flattered (we're always flattered), and I had done my canned "English Department" presentation at Tri-Delt years ago.

I found Tri-Delta, halfway down the winding street tucked between two other faded mansions. It was almost ten o'clock. The lights were on all through the house and the windows and doors thrown open. I walked up the wide steps and into the vestibule. Everyone was at the carnival at this hour and I felt an odd elation standing in the grand and empty house.

This was among the strangest things I have ever done as a college professor—wander into a sorority house. But I did. I went through the living room and up the wooden stairway to the second floor and I went from door to door, reading the nameplates. The doors were all partially open and I could see the chambers in disarray, books scattered on the beds and underthings on the floor. The hallway smelled musty and sweet, and the doors were festooned with collages of clippings and photographs and memorabilia so that many times I had to read the notes to discover whose room it was. It was kind of delicious there in the darkened hallway, sensing that hours ago a dozen young women had dressed and brushed their hair in these rooms.

At the end of the corridor, on a dark paneled door, there were several sheets of white typing paper, and I saw instantly that this was Laurie's room, even before I went close enough to read any of it. It was, of course, Hartwell's poetry. The poem I had seen was taped there, along with five others he had typed and not shown me. Now, however, each was scrawled with red-ink marginalia in the loopy, saccharine handwriting of sorority girls. Their comments were filthy, puerile, and inane. Obscene ridicule. My heart beat against my forehead suddenly, and my eyes burned. Through her open door, I saw Laurie's red plaid kilt on the floor next to a black slip. I felt quite old and quite heavy and very out of place.

I fled. I rattled down the stairway, taking two steps at a time, and across the foyer and back into the night. A couple, arm in arm, were coming through the door. They were drunk and I nearly knocked them over. I recovered and hurried into the dark of Old Tilden Lane, where I found something on my hand, and I released the two balloons.

I am a man who lives in six rooms half a mile from the campus where I teach. I like Chopin, Shostakovich, Courvoisier, and Kona coffee. I have a library of just over two thousand books. After these things, my similarities with Hartwell end. He has his life and I have mine, and he is not like me at all. We are lonely men who teach in college. I'll give you that.

DeRAY

One thing led to another. Liz and I started fixing up our place before the baby came. First the nursery and then wallpaper in the hall and new carpet and then new linoleum and new cabinets in the kitchen and then a new small bay window for the kitchen; and it was through this new window that we would look out upon the lot and silently measure the progress of the weeds.

I was ready to use August to lean back and do a little reading, but you get a woman and an infant standing in a tidy little bay window looking out at a thorny desert and seeing a grassy playground, and you get out the grid paper and sharpen the pencils and start making plans.

A dump truck unloaded nine yards of mountain topsoil. I took delivery of eighteen railroad ties and four hundred and fifty used bricks. I tiered the garden with three levels of ties and laid a brick walkway along the perimeter. I dug the postholes and stained the redwood before I assembled the fence, and then, when I nailed the boards in place—just so along the string line on top— that's when my plan became apparent from the window. It would be a little world, safe, enclosed, where my daughter, when she got around to walking, would tumble in the thick green grass.

It was a dry summer and I'd wait until late in the day when the house could throw its shadow on the project and then I'd plunge out into the heat. Our pup, Burris, wouldn't even go out with me. I was only good for two hours, and then I'd stumble into the house, dehydrated, a crust of dirt on my forehead, my shirt soaked through. Burris would lift his head from the linoleum and then go back to sleep.

Evenings while my strength held, I marched around the yard, pulling my old stepladder loaded with four cinder blocks, leveling the topsoil. I would drag it in slow figure eights through the thick dirt with the rope cutting at my chest like a crude halter. And it was during this time, during my dray-horse days, that my neighbor DeRay would cruise in on his cycle and come to the fence and say, "Hey, good for you, Ace. I'd give you a hand, but I've already got a job. But you know where you can find a beer later."

So I started going over there when I'd feel the first dizziness from the heat. I'd drop the rope and pick my wet shirt away from my chest and walk next door and visit with DeRay.

If I told you that DeRay was a guy who was on parole and loved his motorcycle, it would be misleading, though he did have a big blue tattoo of a skull and a rose. He wore size-thirteen engineer boots and a biker's black cap, greasy as a living thing. In the evenings he arrived home, proud as a man on a horse, yanking the big Harley back onto its stand, and throwing his right leg back over the bike purposefully to come to the ground and stand as a body utterly capable of trouble.

But the picture needs qualification. For instance: it wasn't actually parole. It was *like* parole. Once a month DeRay saw a guy at social services to state that he had not been in any bars. He could not go into a bar for another four months, because he used to be in barroom fights. He would go to biker bars and when a fight would start, he would fight. It was his personality, they told him. He knew none of the people in the fights and the fights weren't about him in any way, but his personality—when it was exposed to a fight, especially indoors—dictated that he fight too. So, it wasn't parole. And he did have that tattoo on the inside of his right forearm, but unless he stopped to show it to you it was hard to tell there was a rose. It looked like a birthmark.

He showed it to me one night on his front porch. Evenings were cool there and that is where he and Krystal sat on an old nappy couch and watched the traffic and drank beer. They drank exactly five six-packs every night, he told me, and—at first—thirty cans seemed a lot, and I worried that there might be a fight, but I came to see that DeRay generally slowed down over the evening, climbing off the porch in those big boots to move his Lawn Jet, or to pack another six beers into the Igloo. Some nights he stood and talked to the traffic. If he started talking like that while I was around, I stood and quietly left. It was his business.

The thing about DeRay that cannot be minimized was his love for his motorcycle. It was a large Harley-Davidson with a beautiful maroon gas tank and chrome fenders. The world was ten miles deep in the reflections. The way he listened to it when he first kicked the starter; the way he kept it running—silent—when he drove away in the morning as if man and machine were being sucked into a vacuum, disappearing down the street; the way he dismounted with clear pleasure—these things showed his affection.

Once Liz was out in front of our garage putting Allie in the stroller when DeRay came up and plucked the baby from her, saying, "Come on over here, baby, check these wheels." He put Allie on the seat of the huge motorcycle and she broke into a real grin. She could see her face in a dozen shiny places. "See," DeRay said to Liz, "she loves it. It won't be long." He called to the porch: "Hey, Krystal, check this out!"

Krystal appeared and leaned over. "Oh, right, DeRay. She's a real mama. She's your new mama, all right."

I watched it all from our new kitchen window, and seeing DeRay there holding the baby on the Harley, I thought: There's the center—the two most loved things on the block.

Both DeRay and Krystal were somewhere in their forties. She was a lean woman who looked good in tight jeans. In the face she resembled Joan Baez, perhaps a little more worn—and her nose was larger, pretty and hawklike at the same time. Her long reddish hair was wired with some gray and she usually wore it all in a bandanna. She told me she was one of four women who were on line crews in the entire state. She made it sound like a lot of fun. I'd sit on their porch, my head full of bubbles anyway with yard fever, dirt, and cold beer. One of my calves would start to tremble, and I imagined if I worked with Krystal she'd always be telling me what to do, like a mother, and I would do it. Her lean face seemed hard and affectionate. It had seen a lot of traffic, that was clear. From the corner of the porch, I could see my new kitchen window—Liz in there moving around the high chair.

One night when I was at DeRay's, Krystal went inside where we could hear her on the phone.. "Her in-laws," DeRay told me. "Old Krystal's had herself a couple of cowboys."

Later, we were just talking when out of the blue he said, "What's the worst thing you ever did?"

I knew that he was going to make some confession, a theft or beating a woman, some threat he'd made stick. He looked hard that night, his face vaguely blue in the early-evening gloom.

"I don't know," I said. "Burn down the ROTC Building." It was an old joke. I was on the roof of the building the night it burned, but I was only peripherally involved in the crime.

"Oh, arsony," DeRay mocked. "That's terrible."

I drank from my beer and went ahead: "What's the worst thing you ever did?"

"What you're doing now."

"What?" I sat up. "What am I doing?"

"Dragging dirt around. Putting in a yard."

"Oh," I said. "I hear that. It's torture."

"No you don't. You don't even know," he said. "I've had three houses. How old do you think I am?"

"I don't know. Forty-five?"

"Forty-nine." He rocked forward and threw his beer can out with the others. "I've had three families, for chrissakes. And that doesn't even count this deal here." He gestured over his shoulder where Krystal was on the phone. He snapped another beer open and grimaced over the first sip: "I mean, I put in some lawns."

"That's a lot of work," I said.

"Nah." He waved it off. "You can't even hear me. But listen, when you dig for the sprinklers, rent a trencher. You won't be sorry."

And DeRay was right. There is nothing better after an unbroken plain or manual labor than to introduce a little technology into the program. The trencher was beautiful. The large treaded tires measured the line exactly and the entire mechanism crawled across my yard like a tortoise. The trench was carved as if with a knife, straight sides and a square bottom exactly eight inches from the surface. All the other feats of the past year, the room in the basement, the kitchen window, my straight fence, vanished before this, the first stage of my sprinkling system. That night I worked way beyond my usual quitting time. When I finally looked up, I saw the yellow light in the kitchen; the world was dark.

This is when DeRay opened the gate and came up and took the handlebars of the trencher out of my hands and conducted it to the end of the line. It was the last ditch. He surveyed the yard and switched the machine off. "Yeah, it's a good, simple machine," he said. "Load it up and come over for a beer."

I stayed at their place until almost eleven. I didn't count as I left, but I knew there were more than thirty empties on the lawn. DeRay receded from the conversation and Krystal told me about her first husband, who was in a mental health facility in Denver, a chronic schizophrenic. She filed to divorce him while he was in the hospital. "He was as crazy as you get to be," she said. "I still keep in touch with his mom and dad in Oklahoma City. He was a dear boy," Krystal said, "but he couldn't keep two things together and his jealousy cost me three jobs."

When I went home all the lights were off. I took my

clothes off in the garage as always and padded in. Liz was in bed watching television. I could hear people laughing. I turned on the bathroom light, and Liz said, "How're the Hell's Angels?"

"You've been watching too much Letterman." I came to the bedroom door.

"You've been outside this house since four o'clock. We had a lovely dinner."

"Oh, now we're going to fight about dinner?" I could feel the rough cuff of dirt around my neck and I hated standing there dirty and naked.

"We're going to fight about whatever I want to fight about."

"Look, Liz. Don't. I've been in the yard. We want the yard, right?" I felt the closeness of the rooms; it was suddenly strange to be inside. "I've got to take a shower," I said.

"Where are you?" she said before I could turn. It was a tough question, because I was right there full of beer, but she was on to something. It was August and I wasn't looking forward to school starting. I shrugged and showed her my brown arms. She looked at me and said, "Let it go, if you like. Just let the yard go."

I bought the controls for the sprinkling system. Opening the boxes on my lap and holding the timer compartment and the bank of valves was wonderful. The instruction booklet was well written: simple and illustrated. I took the whole thing over to DeRay and showed him.

"Yeah," he said, turning the valves over in his hand. "They've got this thing down to the bare minimum and there's a two-week timer." I knew he was a union machinist for Hercules Powder Company, and in the four months he'd been my neighbor he'd told me that three different deals he'd worked up had gone into space on satellites. "You're going to be the King of Irrigation with this thing."

Though Liz didn't like the idea, I put the control box on the guestroom wall downstairs. It took me two six-packs. She said it didn't look right, a sprinkler system timer box on the guestroom wall. I said some things too, including the fact that it was the only wall I could put it on. She just shrugged.

I finished at three o'clock in the morning. I went out in the garage and filled the spreader and spread the lawn seed all across the yard first one way and then the other in a complete checkerboard just like it said on the package. It was quiet in the neighborhood and I tried to step lightly through the raked topsoil. There was no traffic on the streets and the darkness was even and phosphorescent as I walked back and forth. It seemed like the time of night to spread your lawn seed.

The next morning, Liz woke me with a nudge from her foot. I was asleep on the floor in the nursery. "Who are you?" she said.

"We're all done," I said. "The yard's all done."

"Great," she said, carrying Allie into the kitchen. "Looks like we drank some beer last night. Did we have a good time? I think you've caught a little beer fever from your good buddy next door. This is being a hard summer on you."

Very late that night, Burris began barking and Allie woke and started crying. "What is it?" Liz said from her side of the bed.

"Nothing. It's okay," I said. There was a strange noise

in the house, a low moan in the basement, which I understood immediately was the water pipes. I went to Allie
and changed her diaper. She was awake by that time so I
carried her into the kitchen, where Burris was jumping
at the window. I had set the system to start at four-thirty,
which it now was, and outside the window the sprinklers,
whispering powerfully, sprayed silver into the dark. I sat
down and Allie crawled up over my shoulder to watch
the waterworks. Burris stood at the window on two legs
humming nervously. I swallowed and felt how tired I was,
but there was something mesmerizing about the water
darkening the soil in full circles. A moment later, the first
bank of sprinklers shrank and went off and the second
row sputtered and came on full, watering every inch I'd
planned. It was a beautiful thing.

There were five banks, each set for twenty minutes,
and when the last series—outside the fence—kicked on, I
saw a problem. The heads were watering not only my
strip of yard, but the sidewalk and part of the street. Along
the driveway, they were spraying well over my strip, and
DeRay's motorcycle was dripping in the gray light.

I stood so sharply that Allie whimpered, and I took her
quickly in to Liz and laid her in the bed. I put on my robe
and grabbed a towel, and I went outside. It was a little
after five and I wiped down the bike until the towel was
sopping, and then I used the corner of my robe on the
spokes and rims, and I was down on my knees when I
heard voices and two high school girls in tennis clothes
walked by swinging their rackets. It was full light. I looked
up and saw Liz in the kitchen window. Her face was clear
to me. There was grit in my knees and my feet were cold.

"I'm going to have to adjust those last heads," I told
her when I went inside.

"Why don't you make some coffee first," Liz said. She was sitting at the table. Allie was back in her crib asleep.

"You want to talk about what's going on?" Liz said. I poured coffee into the filter and set it on the carafe.

"There's too much pressure this early," I said with my back to her. "We soaked DeRay's motorcycle."

"You're taking care of DeRay's motorcycle now?" she said. "You're going to get arrested exposing yourself to schoolgirls."

After a long tired moment of standing staring at the dripping coffee, I poured a cup while it was still brewing and set it in front of my wife. "Look, Liz, everything's fine." I opened my hand to show the kitchen, the window, the yard. "And now the grass is going to grow."

That evening there was a knock at the kitchen door just after six. Liz answered it and when she didn't come back to watch the news, I went out and found her talking to DeRay on the back porch. "Hello, Ace," he said to me.

"DeRay has invited us to . . ." Liz smiled. "What is it, DeRay?"

"They're testing one of our engines and I've got passes. We could make it a picnic."

Liz looked at me blankly, no clue, so I just said, "Let's do it. Sounds good. This is one of your engines?"

"We did some work on it. It's no big deal, but we can go up above the plant in the hills and get off the homestead for a while, right?"

"Right," I said, looking at Liz. "A picnic."

The Saturday of our picnic dawned gray—high clouds that mocked the end of summer. I offered to make the lunch, but Liz nudged me aside and made turkey sand-wiches and put nectarines and iced tea and a six-pack of Olympia in the cooler along with a big bowl of her pasta salad. When I saw the beer I realized that she was going to do this right by the rules and then when it turned into a tragedy or simple misery or some mistake, she would have her triumph. She had never bought a six-pack of Olympia before in her life.

At eleven, we met DeRay and Krystal in our driveway. She was wearing a bright blue bandanna on her head. DeRay lifted his orange ice chest into the back of our Volvo and said, "Now follow us."

Before we were down the block, Liz said, "We're not driving like that."

"It's his right to change lanes," I said, moving left. "He's using his signals."

"We've got a baby in the car."

"Liz," I said, "I know we've got a baby in the car. And we're following DeRay out to Hercules Powder for a picnic. This is going to be a nice day."

As it turned out, DeRay made the light at Thirteenth and we didn't. He disappeared ahead, the blue bandanna on Krystal's head dipping in front of two cars in the dis-tance, and they were gone. We sat in silence. Allie was humming as if she had something to say and would say it next. There was no traffic on Thirteenth at all. How long is a traffic light? I've never known.

When the light turned green, Liz said: "Just let us out."

"Good," I said. "Where would I do that?"

"Right here," she said.

Without hesitation, instantly, I pulled against the curb. The sudden stop made Allie exhale with a high, sweet squeal. "Is this good?" I said.

Liz looked at me with a face I'd never seen before. She unlocked her door and unbuckled her seat belt.

"Wait," I said. I knew I was out of control. "I'll drop you at Claire's. Shut your door."

She snapped her door closed, but did not refasten her seat belt. I wheeled sharply back onto the street and dropped three blocks down to her sister's house. I jumped out and ran around to the baby's door and lifted her out. I kissed her and placed her in Liz's arms and went back around to my door. I didn't want any more talking. It was like the things I've done when I was drunk. Before I could measure anything, I was back on the access headed for West Valley.

I just thought about driving, how I would pass each car, dip right, reassume my lane, and head out. When I entered the freeway, I hammered the Volvo to maximum speed. I hated this car. It had always been too heavy and too slow.

DeRay waited for me at the main gates of Hercules, the plant situated alone on the vast gradual slope of the west valley. There was a guard at the gate, and DeRay waved me through, grinning, and then he and Krystal shot past me through the empty parking lot and under the red-checked water tower to the corner of the pavement where they dropped onto a smooth dirt road that wound up the hill. Powdery dust lifted from their tires and they led me up the lane and around into a small gravel parking area where there were already four blue government vans. Off to the side about twenty people, about half of them in military khaki, stood in the weeds. DeRay parked his bike and came over to where I was getting out of the Volvo.

"Where's the wife?" he said, looking in. "Is the baby here?"

"No, they decided to go to Liz's sister's."

"Oh hell, that's too bad. This should be good."

We carried the coolers and a blanket to a high spot in the dry grass and spread out our gear. "Who are those guys?" I asked.

"The staff and some guys from Hill Air Force Base."

"Is it okay to have a beer?"

"That's why we brought it." He reached inside the orange Igloo for the cold cans and handed me a beer. Krystal wasn't drinking.

DeRay walked down a few yards to look at the bunker a half mile below. I had forgotten the view from out here. I could see the whole city against the Wasatch Range and each of the blue canyons: Little Cottonwood, Big Cottonwood, Millcreek. On the hill I could see the old white Ambassador Building, two blocks from my house, and I could imagine my yard, the fence.

Krystal was staring out over the valley. "Your wife didn't want to come to the country?" she said. I could tell that she knew all about it.

DeRay came back. "It's all set. In twenty minutes, you're going to hear some noise." He pointed to the bunker. It'll fire south. They'll catch this on the university seismograph as a two-point. What'd you bring to eat?"

We broke out the sandwiches and the salad. DeRay sat down on the blanket, Indian-style, his big boots like furniture beneath him, and ate hungrily. "Hey, this is good," he said, pointing his fork at the pasta salad. "Nothing like a picnic." He drained his beer and tossed it over his shoulder into the tall grass. "Just like home," he said. While we ate, DeRay had waved at a couple of the guys by the vans, and later when we were cleaning up the paper plates, one man walked up to us.

"How does it look?" DeRay asked him as they shook hands.

"Good, Ace. We've got a countdown."

DeRay introduced us to the man, Clint, and we all stood in a line facing the bunker. "In a minute you are going to see thirty seconds of the largest controlled explosion in the history of this state," DeRay said to me and winked. "We hope."

A moment later I saw the group near the vans all take a step backward and then we saw the flash at the earthen mound become a huge white flare in a roar that seemed to flatten the grass around us. It was too bright to look at and hard to look away from, and the sound was ferocious, a pressure. I found myself turning my head to escape it, but there was no help. Clint wore sunglasses and was staring at the flash itself. He wasn't moving. Round balls of smoke rolled from the flame and began to tumble into the air, piling in a thick black column. Krystal watched with her head tilted. She was squinting and her mouth was open.

When it stopped, it stopped so suddenly it was as if someone had closed a door on it, and the roar was sucked out of the air and replaced by a tinny buzzing which I realized was in my ears.

"Jesus Christ," Krystal said.

The people by the vans were kind of cheering and calling and several of them turned and pointed at DeRay happily.

"Congratulations, Ace," Clint said and shook DeRay's hand again. "It was beautiful."

"Yeah, right," DeRay said. "Now on to phase four."

Clint walked down to where the group was boarding the vans, and two more guys came up and shook DeRay's hand, and then the four vans packed up and drove carefully down the dirt road out of sight. I was watching the smoke cloud twist and roll silently in the sky, thick as oil. You could see this from our house. I wondered what Liz was doing, what she had told her sister. My ears simmered. With the vans gone this seemed a lonely place.

"That was your rocket?" I asked him.

"Fuel feed. I'm the fuel feed guy."

I looked at him. "I thought you were a machinist."

"That's all it is, really." He pulled out another beer and sat on the cooler. "Just like this can. Same problem. You've got to keep the beer under pressure—two or three atmospheres. But you've got to cut the top here so I can open it with one finger. How deep do you score it? Figure that out and your problems are history." He lifted the tab and the beer hissed. He took a long swig and shrugged. "Oly's a good beer, right? We're having a fine picnic here. Am I right?"

Krystal walked toward us, arms folded.

DeRay said, "Hey, let's not head out yet." He stood. "Ace, you feel like riding the bike? I feel like a little ride." He turned to the woman. "You okay, Krystal, if we run up the hill for a minute? You can have some more of that great macaroni salad."

He started the Harley and I climbed on behind him. "Your wife is some cook. I'm sorry she missed this."

We cruised slowly down the road and through the lot. I was thinking about Liz and I felt bad and I could feel it getting worse. And it was funny, but I wanted it worse.

When we hit the highway, DeRay turned and said, "My second wife could cook," and he jammed the accelerator and we were lost in the wind, going seventy up the old road toward Copperton, slowing through Bingham and then hitting it hard again, winding up the canyon using both sides of the road. It didn't matter. The air was at me like a hatchet and I'd watch the yellow line drift under the bike on one side and then another. At the top, the gate to the mine was closed. The mine had been closed for years.

DeRay pulled up to the gate and I felt the dizzy pressure of stopping. "I come up here all the time," he said. "After work I just drive up. Push the gate." The chain was locked, but it opened three feet. He conducted the motorcycle under the chain easily. Near the pit, we sped up a paved incline and circled into the parking lot of the old visitors' center.

The structure was weathered. The back walls of the shelter held poster-size framed photographs of the mining operations: a dynamite blast, the ore train in a tunnel, one of the giant trucks being filled by a mammoth loader. DeRay had gone to the overlook and was leaning on the rail staring out at the vast rock amphitheater. The clouds above the copper mine were moving and shredding. The wind was chilly. "You want to bring the bike in?" I asked him. "We're going to get wet."

"Forget it," he said.

"I hope Krystal gets in the car."

"That woman knows what to do in the rain." He stood and pointed at four deer that walked along the uppermost level of the mine. "Check that."

"What are they looking for?" I said. The animals had made some kind of mistake.

DeRay leaned on the rail and said, "You know that Krystal's leaving."

"What?"

"Yeah, she has to go. Her crazy man is on leave. He's

out. They weren't really divorced. You can't divorce someone who's crazy. Something. She's going out to his folks'."

"I didn't know. Hey, I'm sorry."

"Come on, what is it? She has to go," he said. DeRay rubbed his eyes with a thumb and forefinger. His face in the dim light looked blue, the way it did some nights on his porch. When he looked up, he said, "Hey, look at you." I reached up and felt my hair standing all over. "You're going to want to get a cap." DeRay lifted his and snugged it on my head. "Why don't you take it for a spin? Go ahead, down the road and back." He waved at the motorcycle and his tattoo in the gloom looked like a wound.

I said, "Krystal's a good woman."

"Oh hell," he said. "They're all good women."

"Things happen," I said.

He turned to me. "No they don't. I know all about this. Things don't *happen*. I'm an engineer. One thing leads to another. Listen. You're a nice kid, but that fence around your place won't stop a thing. What are you, thirty?"

We could smell the rain. It felt real late. It felt like October, November. When you have a baby, you have to put in a lawn. You're supposed to build a fence. There's no surprise in that. I am like every other man in that.

"That was some rocket," I said. I could taste trouble in my mouth and I felt kind of high, like a kid a long way from home. "I'm sorry Liz didn't see it. It won't be easy to describe."

DeRay pointed again at the deer and we watched as they tried to scramble up the steep mine slope. It was desperate but so far away that we couldn't hear the gravel falling. They kept slipping. Finally, two made it and disappeared over the summit. The two left behind stood still.

"Hey, don't listen to me," DeRay said. "I'm just squawking. We should have brought some beer."

I went out and mounted the Harley. It came up off the stand easier than I thought and started right up. I sat down in the seat and looked over at DeRay as the wheels crept forward. I could sense the ion charge before rain. We were definitely going to get wet. Just a little spin.

DeRay was right. He had been right about the trencher and he was right about one thing leading to another. I am not the kind of person who stays out in bad weather, but there I was. I lifted my feet from the pavement and felt it all happen. It was a big machine, more than I could handle, but I could just feel it wanting to balance. It began to drift. I'd never felt anything like it before. There were accidents in this thing. I would just take it down to the gate and right back up again.

BLAZO

When Burns arrived in Kotzebue, they were shooting the dogs. He'd never been to Alaska before and it seemed without compromise. Weather had kept him in Nome for two days, where he'd seen a saloon fire. He'd been across the street in a shop buying chocolate and bottled water, and the eerie frozen scene mesmerized him. As the flames pulsed from both windows in the sharp wind and the crews sprayed water which caked on the wooden structure instantly as ice, the patrons emerged slowly, their collars up in the weather, drinks in their gloved hands. Burns wasn't drinking. He sipped water and ate chocolate in his hotel room, listening to the wind growl. Then the short hop over to Kotzebue was the roughest flight of his life, the plane pitching and dropping, smacking against the treacherous air. Burns could hear dogs barking in the front hold and they helped. It's a short flight, he thought, and they wouldn't crash with dogs.

In Kotzebue, Burns waited in the small metal terminal until a wizened, leather-faced Inuit came up to him and grinned, showing no teeth, and lifted his suitcase into the back of an orange International pickup. Burns followed the man and got into the truck. The cab was rife with the smell of bourbon and four or five bottles rolled around Burns's feet. The man smiled again, his eyes merry, and drove onto the main road of the village, where they fell behind the sheriff's white truck. There were two men in the back with rifles riding in the cold. Kotzebue was gray under old drifts but the wind had ripped the tops from some of the banks and spread new whiter fans of snow across the road. The high school was letting out and three-wheelers and snow machines cruised along the road, both sides, and cut the corners at every crossroad.

Suddenly, the two men in the sheriff's truck stood and raised their rifles, shooting into a field behind the buildings. Each shot twice and then they quickly clambered out of the vehicle as it stopped. One of the men fell to the ice and got back up and followed his partner running into the field.

"What's going on?" Burns asked, but his driver only squinted at him and shook his head slightly. Burns could see the two men standing over a dark form in the snow. He saw one of them shoot again. The man behind the wheel of the sheriff's truck lifted a hand, but Burns's driver did not wave back.

Two streets later, the orange International turned into a narrow off street and stopped in front of an ice-coated trailer. The man unloaded the suitcase and held out four fingers. The way he tapped them made Burns understand.

"Miss Munson will be back at four?"

The man nodded and reached behind Burns and opened the trailer's door. Whiskey, Burns thought, as he watched the man return to the truck and drive off. A thick drift of whiskey moved with the man. As Burns lifted his bag and turned to the iced steps, a black Newfoundland on a chain rose from a doghouse half buried in the snow, shook, and looked up expectantly. It took Burns a moment to recognize the dog, and then he knelt down and ran his hand through the fur. "Molly, you pup," he said. "You grew up." There was a muffled clamor from the roadway and Burns turned to see a passenger fall from a three-wheeler, slide along on his back for ten yards, then climb back on behind the driver. It had begun to snow faintly in the early afternoon, and the tiny dots of frozen snow were sparse in the gloom. Burns scratched the dog again. "Molly," he said. "What happened to Alec?"

In the close warmth of the trailer, Burns again found himself craving food. The cold left him ravenous. In Nome after his daily walks he would fall upon his stash of chocolate like a schoolboy. And now, he barely took time to hang his gear in the small mud room and sit at the table in the kitchen before he was stuffing the candy into his mouth. It was amusing to be so aware of his body after so many years.

There was a stomping, felt more than heard, and Burns saw light in the entry as the door opened and closed. "Hello!" a man's voice called, and a large bearded man in a blue military parka came into the kitchen, pulling off his glove and extending a hand to Burns. "You picked one hell of a week," the man said, shaking Burns' hand. "Glen Batton. I'm the Forest Service here, and," he added in another tone, "a friend of Julie's."

Burns said his name and Glen Batton went ahead with the weather report about a new Siberian front moving in. "If it cleared, I'd fly you out to Kolvik myself. As is, you'll be lucky to get down to the Co-op for candy." Batton pointed to the candy wrappers on the table. "I'm sorry about your son."

Burns nodded.

"You're from Connecticut."

"Yes. Connecticut."

Glen Batton put his glove back on. "Well, listen, I just wanted to introduce myself and offer my services, though that may be useless. How long are you here?"

"I'm not sure," Burns said. "I need to get out to Kolvik."

"Well, you won't do that," Glen said, moving back to the door. "But have a nice visit. I'll probably see you Friday at the hospital party."

"Why are the police shooting the dogs?"

"Strays," Batton said. "Too many loose dogs raising hell with the teams. Count the dogs in this town sometime." He turned to leave, but came back into the room. "Hey, listen. You may need to know a couple of things." Batton brushed the parka hood off his long hair, "Look, what happened to Alec is a bad deal, but it happens all the time. People don't understand this country. They think they can handle it, but you can't handle it."

"I see," Burns said.

"And I should tell you this." Glen Batton looked quickly away and back. "Julie is a little fragile about this whole deal. Your visit a year after it all happened. We've talked about it. I don't know what your plans are, but you may want to step lightly."

"I will."

"If it gets tight, you can always bunk with me or at the hotel."

"Thank you. I'll remember that," Burns said, holding

Glen's look until the bearded man turned and left. Now he wanted a drink, blood sugar or no blood sugar; Burns could feel the call in his gut, his heartbeat, the roof of his mouth. He went to the sink and drew and drank three glasses of water.

Burns heard a fuss outside and then the clatter of claws on the linoleum of the entry and the Newfoundland came bounding in and burrowed his nose into Burns's hand where it hung beside the easy chair in which he slept. He had sat down to read in the small living room and sleep had taken him like an irrefutable force. Now a woman appeared in the entrance, and that was Burns's first thought: She's not a girl. He had last seen his son Alec six years ago when he had graduated college in New Haven. Burns had expected his wife to be a girl. Julie removed her knee-length lavender parka and the white knit cap and shook her hair, smiling at him. Without meaning to, Burns stared frankly at her in her white nurse's dress. It was the first surprise he'd had since he'd been in Alaska: Julie was a woman, a tall woman with pale blond hair that fell below her shoulders. He stood and took her hand.

"What are you smiling at?" she said, and smiled. "Sit down, Tom. I'm going to call you Tom, okay? I'm glad you're here. How was your flight?" Burns felt things shifting. First all the hunger, and then the nap taking him like a kid, and now this woman in white.

"I fell asleep," he said. "Sorry."

"It's too warm in here." Julie went to the thermostat. "That's the one thing about Alaska. It's too warm all the time. There's no such thing as a little cold. They keep the hospital at eighty degrees. It reminds me of Manhattan that way." She sat on the couch and took off her shoes. "Alec talked about you quite a lot. And so did Helen, but you're quite different than I pictured."

"Oh?"

She stood up, her dress rustling. "You want a drink?"

"Water's fine."

"That's right. I knew that. Sorry." Burns watched her splash some Wild Turkey into a plastic tumbler. "Okay, I'll be right back. I've got to get these stockings off. Yes, from Helen I imagined you'd be a bit wrecked or frumpy, you know, dirty overcoat, greasy hair."

"Bottle of tokay?"

"I'm kidding, but your ex-wife can be a bit severe."

"Helen is a woman with a memory."

Julie went down a short hallway where Burns could see the edge of a bed. When he saw her dress fall upon the bed, he stood and moved to the kitchen sink, poured a glass of water, and tried to see out the frosted window. He felt agitated. He pressed the glass against his lip. He was deeply hungry again and he felt funny about falling asleep. Napping wasn't his custom, but the sweet closed warmth of the trailer and the wind heaving at the structure, rocking it faintly, had just taken him. He had been doing things by will for ten years now, since the first week after his forty-second birthday, and he was known as a measured man who had placed the remaining components of his life back together purposefully. He was a man who didn't feel things instantly, and now there was this person, Julie, whom he instantly felt quite wonderful about, and suddenly his mission seemed strange and he felt far from home.

She returned in a worn pair of brown corduroys and a simple white turtleneck. His room was at the other end of the trailer, and as she laid out some towels, Burns couldn't take his eyes from her.

"Blazo picked you up all right?" she said.

"The talkative soul? The whiskey person?"

As she moved about the room, showing him the bureau and the electric blanket control and the closet, he studied her long arms, her wristwatch, her short, unpolished fingernails, the small gold necklace, the rise of her collarbones under the fabric of her pullover.

"He can't talk. He drank some heating fuel years ago. Blazo. He drank some Blazo and doesn't talk, but he's a gem. He is the mechanic to trust in this village."

Julie had pale green eyes and a faint spray of freckles across her nose and forehead. Burns put her at about thirty. He felt like a teenager sneaking looks at her breasts. He hadn't seen a woman in a turtleneck sweater for twenty years. There was an angry red scar on her neck protuding from her shirt, which stunned him at first, and then he realized it was a violin mark. Alec had had one.

Burns heard two concussions from outside and then two more, the distant snapping of gunfire. He held on to the sink and felt the wind pull at the trailer and he thought: Don't touch her. Don't you touch this woman.

For dinner Julie had a white cloth on the kitchen table and Burns tried to eat slowly. "I appreciate your putting me up like this," he said. "I'm genuinely sorry we haven't met until now."

"Tom, don't start apologizing. I mean it. This is Alaska, there isn't room." Julie looked at him squarely. "I understand about the wedding and Alec did too. Believe me. And you were right not to come. It was Helen's show really." She sipped her bourbon, then lifted a finger from the rim and pointed at him. "I'm not kidding."

"I just want to see where he lived out there, where he . . . I missed so much, and now I just want to see what it's like here."

"This is what it's like, dark and windy, lots of accidents."

"I spoke with Helen before I came and she simply wanted you to know that she would love to hear from you and that if you ever needed anything she would help. She was quite sincere."

Julie placed her glass carefully on the table. "I know. We've spoken about the funeral. He wasn't my husband anymore, of course. We were only married the one year. And I hadn't seen him for months. I tried to handle everything I could at this end, but I couldn't go down to the states and get all involved in a world which wasn't there anymore. You went out?"

"I did," Burns said. "I finally went to something."

Burns ate slowly, his hunger a fire that had him on the edge of his chair. He felt oddly alert. "Who found Alec?"

"Glen reported the cabin burn on his return from a caribou count, and the Search and Rescue went out from here. You can see Lloyd tomorrow, the sheriff. It was his men."

They were quiet for a while, Burns eating and watching Molly, chin down on the living-room rug, watch him. All of these things had happened, Alec's wedding, divorce, death, in half a dog's life.

"So, you're Thomas Burns," Julie said, smiling again. "It is just a little weird to see you."

"That's the way everybody seems to be taking it."

"Well, Glen is convinced you're a cop." She pointed at his clean plate. "Still hungry?"

"No," he lied. He stood and set his dishes in the sink. "Is there need for a cop?"

She joined him at the counter and spoke softly. "No. It's an unhappy story, but we've got all the cops we need." She stopped him from clearing the table. "Come on, I'd better take you down to the Tahoe before my students get here. All visitors go to the Tahoe. The largest bar in the Arctic Circle. Even though you don't drink, it's a good walk, and next week in Darien, you can say you've seen it once, tell stories."

Outside in the heavy wind, Burns and Julie shuffled along the hard snowpacked roadway. The dark was gashed by several flaring arc lights above the armory and the high school, new brick buildings built with the first oil surplus money. Several vehicles passed them at close range, snow machines and three-wheelers bulleting by, and as Burns shied from them, he bumped Julie several times, saying, "Sorry, I'm not used to this."

"It's all right. They're not either," she said, pointing to the way the small vehicles cut the corners at every intersection, their paths running across open yards and slicing very close to the buildings. The drivers wouldn't slow down at all around these shortcuts. Burns cringed watching them disappear. They'll be killed, he thought. They'll crash head-on with someone coming the other way and be killed. He and Julie didn't speak in the pressure of the cold. They stopped several times to pick things from the roadway: a scarf, a big leather mitten, and at the corner where they turned for the bar, a loaf of bread, still soft. He found such litter alarming, but Julie only smiled and told him simply, "Bring it along."

The Tahoe was a large metal building which looked like a one-story warehouse. Julie led him up the iced steps and across the wide porch into the big barroom. Inside the door, in the dark, one booth was stacked high with miscellaneous gear: sweaters, hats, and gloves. Julie told him, "Put your treasures right there. It's the lost and found." The vast room was gloomy and crowded. As Burns's eyes adjusted, he saw that the booths were full of Inuit, and though the room was warm and redolent of cigarettes and fur, few people had taken their coats off.

"What would you like?" Julie said.

"I'd like a vanilla shake," Burns said. "This country has got me starved. But I'll take a soda water, anything really."

It was not an animated bar. Burns could see four school board members who were on his flight standing at the bar, talking, but they were the loudest group. The dark clusters of natives huddled around the tables and booths in the room spoke quietly if at all. Even the pool players moved with a kind of lethargy. Burns stood by the end of the bar, his stomach growling as he thawed. He'd been in lots of bars and this was possibly the largest. In the old days, after martinis at his club, he'd hit every hole in the wall on the way to Grand Central, eventually taking the last train to Connecticut, the ride as cloudy and smeared as the windows. He hadn't been a sloppy drunk; he'd been a careful drunk. The word was "serious"—for everything he'd done, really. He was a serious young man, who had married seriously and become a serious attorney, who drank seriously and became a serious drunk. The mistakes he made were serious and now, in the Arctic Circle, he thought of himself in the Tahoe as a serious visitor on a serious mission who did not drink and took his not drinking seriously. He knew how he was perceived and it was a kind of comfort for Burns to have the word to hold on to.

"Welcome to Alaska," Julie said, handing him a glass of sparkling water. "There are no limes." She touched his glass with her own.

"I'd worry if there were."

"You don't drink," she said, sipping her whiskey. "Smart man."

"No. Alec I'm sure told you. I got smart a little late." He sucked on his lip and nodded at her. "I've missed a lot. I'm an *old* man."

"Not quite." She smiled and touched his glass again. "And it is a world of accidents, believe me. Someone just dropped the bread, right? And on the way home we'll find the peanut butter. Lots of things get dropped." She looked at his face appraisingly. "You're still a smart man." Julie waved a hand out over the room. "How do you like the Tahoe, the hub of culture on the frontier?"

"It's big. I spent a lot of time having stronger drinks in smaller places."

"You're a lawyer."

"I am. I was a good lawyer years ago. Now I'm simply highly paid: probate on the Gold Coast. Did Alec say he'd forgiven me for it?"

"Alec always spoke of you in the best terms. You taught him how to sail?"

"One summer a long time ago. I wasn't around much."

Someone, a figure, fell out of a booth across the room and two tablemates stood and lifted the person back into place.

"Will you stay here?" Burns asked her. "In Kotzebue?"

"I'm a nurse. There's a lot of call for that here. I've got a life—and I've got my students."

The walk back to the trailer again awakened in Burns a huge hunger. He had the same feeling he always had when he spoke of his past, honest and diminished, but now he mainly felt hungry. The wind was in their faces and they leaned against it, talking, while Burns felt the chocolate bar in his pocket. Julie spoke of meeting his son their year at Juilliard. "I wasn't their kind of musician," she said, punching the words into the wind. "I was lucky. I'd been lucky with the competitions really. And I didn't really care for all the work. It was nonstop." They could hear dogs barking out in the fields where the teams were staked. Julie took his arm and turned into the narrow, icy lane where her trailer stood. "I like to play—I teach and I still play—but at Juilliard, well," she faced him in the cold dark, her face luminous, "too many *artists.*"

Inside the trailer, Julie's three students plucked at violin strings tuning their instruments. She introduced them to Burns: Tara, Mercy, and Calvin, native kids all about twelve. They sat serious and straight-backed in the living room for the lesson while Julie began leading them through the half hour's exercises. Calvin's eyes kept going sideways to Burns, and Burns could see they were all self-conscious, so he stood and started for his room. Julie stopped and came to him. "Can I get you anything?"

"No, thank you," he said. Taking off his coat had made him impossibly tired. "I'll see you in the morning."

As he climbed into bed he could hear the sliding harmonies of the four violins rise and fall. Alec had started the violin when he was six, the year Helen had taken him and gone back to Ohio, and years later when Alec finished Juilliard, he had gone to Alaska to teach. Burns had never contacted his son when he was studying in New York. In those days guilt had slowed everything Burns did. He had moved his practice to Connecticut by then, and three times Burns had taken the train into the city and walked by the music school, slowing enough to hear the strains of piano or French horn from a window. And then as if scolded by the music, he hurried away. He couldn't cross the street and go in. Now Burns cringed at his cowardice.

Under the heavy blankets in his room, as the wind moaned over the trailer, Burns listened to the violins. He'd eaten his chocolate and was tired to his bones. He could feel the structure moving in the weight of the gusts. It was like being aboard ship.

Later he had heard voices, their timbre, something almost angry, and then he felt the door shut, and the rushing quiet took him again.

Burns woke in the bright morning and heard the white wind. He was disappointed as he wiped at the frost on the inside of his window to see the storm outside, but there was something else: all this weather. He liked this odd place, big on the earth and full of weather. He'd had the same feeling on certain days sailing off St. Johns: the ocean could be a big, unknowable thing there, indifferent to anybody's plans.

Julie had left him a map on the table, a pencil grid of the village with arrows to the sheriff's office and his phone number. At the bottom it said, "I'll be back at five—and then I'd better take you to the hospital party, so everyone can meet the mystery man. It's at seven. J." Beside it was a large sweet roll, which Burns wolfed down with a mug of the cold powdered milk from the fridge. Standing there in his pajamas in the kitchen drinking the thick, cold milk, Burns grinned. He felt like a kid. He was grinning. Powdered milk was better than he had imagined.

Outside, marching sidelong into the killer wind, Burns felt the cold only in his exposed forehead and then not as cold, but as a constriction, a tight band of pain. He walked with his head turned for protection into his parka hood, and the drivers of the snow machines who roared past also drove with their heads turned. It made him stop and move aside several times. He saw several more mittens in the snow, but didn't pick them up. The day, the world, was all wind, even the rustle of his coat was lost in the gale.

The sheriff's office was two long blocks past the Tahoe in a small complex of state and federal buildings, one-story brick cottages linked by covered walkways. The sheriff was waiting for him, but after they shook hands, Burns had to sit down for a moment and rub his forehead while the aching subsided. He'd sat behind his own desk just like this, rubbing his head, unable to talk to some client as a low wave of nausea rinsed through. In those days, while he tried to poison himself with it, drinking pernicious amounts of gin every night, his clients never knew, his business never quivered. When he went down, they didn't find him for a week, and when Helen came to the hospital, she simply said to stop it, that she was fine and would be, but that killing himself would make it worse for everyone. "You've broken me," she said. "I'm taking the baby and going home." And that was that. He was two weeks in the hospital, having almost lost toes to frostbite, and when he came out, he moved the office to New

Canaan, dropped everything but probate, and knew—essentially—and this had nothing to do with the drinking—that his life was over. Helen had already taken Alec back to Ohio, where her mother had lived, and a few years later she married Charley, an attorney in Chagrin Falls.

The sheriff's name was Lloyd Right, a man all in khaki, whom Burns liked right away. "Mr. Burns," he said, taking Burns's coat and pointing out the easy chair, "now tell me exactly the objectives of your visit to the frozen north."

He nodded through the tale, his jaw in his fist, and then when Burns finished, Lloyd Right stood and went to the three-drawer file in the corner and pulled out a folder. "It doesn't appear as if Glen Batton or anybody else is going to be able to lift you out there." Right went back to his desk and sat down, placing the folder squarely in front of him. "This weather has been tight for a week, and it's a pity, not that there's much to see, but I understand too well the importance of just being at the scene." Right dialed the phone and then hung up. It rang and he picked up and said, "Jerry, bring us two coffees." He looked at Burns. "You want some coffee, don't you?"

"I do."

"Anyway, Julie told me about you and about Alec's mother. These things are always bad. What I can do for you is tell you what I know, let you read the file. It was an accident, you can tell his mother that. We don't have any photos. But Julie had been by his place and she can describe it to you. You could tell the family that you went out there, that—"

"No, I couldn't," Burns said. "I couldn't do that. You understand. I am the family. I could tell Alec's mother I was here and saw this file and that I spoke to you."

The deputy came in with the coffee, setting the two mugs on the sheriff's desk and backing out. While the office door was open, another officer came in, the cold on him like an odor, a rifle in his hand. "Lloyd, they've seen the stray out at the foothills. You coming?"

"Take Bob. Call me in half an hour," Right said. When the men had left, the sheriff sipped his coffee. "We've got one goddam stray left, and he's a smart one. What a lone dog can do to a staked team. You don't want to see it. Some of our teams are worth thousands; two teams are going down for the Iditarod next month. Do they hear about the Iditarod in Connecticut, Mr. Burns?"

"They do," Burns said. "You don't think I can get out to Kolvik?"

"I don't. It's too bad. I've been to the site. Alec lived about two miles from the village, south, in the low hills. The cabin had been totally consumed." The sheriff stood and came around his metal desk, sitting on the edge of the short bookshelf near Burns. "You know, even before he left here, something had happened to Alec," he said. "He had a breakdown or something. This is not in the report. But he began acting strange. You can ask Julie about it. We were sorry about it here. What he had done for the music program in the high school in two years was wonderful, and when he dropped out and moved out there sixty miles, well, everybody felt bad. But we see this kind of thing here. A guy moves out and then further out and moves, if he can, to what he sees as the end of the road, the edge, and either he lives there or he doesn't, but he doesn't come back."

Lloyd Right went back and sat behind his desk, working his closed eyes with his fingers for a moment. He went on, "You figure it. He was a fine musician. So, he moves out to Kolvik and starts a trapline. It was just above the cabin in a draw. That's where they found the body. It was a classic case of freezing to death, I mean, he'd taken off his clothes and they were scattered around. It's very common, Mr. Burns, and I would think it's important that you know this was an accident, not suicide. He misjudged the time and was out too long." Lloyd Right stood again and drained his coffee. "We found the dog out there with him. Julie has her."

On the way home, Burns felt his mouth dry with hunger and he went into the small Co-op and bought a bag of chocolate bars. Outside a man had fallen on the steps and Burns and a woman helped the man climb back up. Burns took the back street to Julie's, the wind now pushing him along the pathway. There were fewer close calls with snow machines here, and he ate the candy and walked slowly, his hands thrust deeply into his parka pockets. Then a strange thing happened that scared him so badly he involuntarily ducked and nearly fell. At first Burns thought something had hit him, but then he saw the light change, a sunflash that settled on the village for a second dropping thick blue shadows on the sides of things. It was painfully bright. The sun was out. In the sky Burns could see the contours of individual clouds. Stay there, he thought. Just stay there.

The party that night was held in the hospital recreation room, a small square room lined with blue vinyl couches. The hospital was obviously an old wooden military building that had been superficially redone. There was a new checkerboard linoleum floor, but wooden-framed windows lined each wall. Julie took Burns by the arm and they went around to everybody in the room, thirty or so people: Julie's head nurse, Karen; Lloyd Right and his wife; both deputies; several nurses and two doctors (both women); Glen Batton; the high school principal and his wife; a dozen teachers there; the school board members whom Burns recognized from his flight; a social counselor named Victor (the only Inuit at the party); some guys from the National Guard; and part of the airport staff. Burns wasn't very comfortable. He'd slept all afternoon and his feet hurt and his face felt swollen. But he was keen, too, because the weather had changed—there was talk of a clearing. Jets were coming in from Nome tomorrow.

He stood by the buffet table and ate strips of the salty ham while he filled a small paper plate with deviled eggs. He felt a bit foolish, but he could not move away from the buffet table, eating handfuls of the chips and dip and mixed nuts, nodding at people with his mouth full, smiling, absolutely out of control. When one of the airport personnel came up and said, "So, you're not a cop," Burns just smiled at him too and shook his head, popping another of the tangy eggs into his mouth.

There was a slide show. One of the nurses had been in the Grand Canyon the past summer and showed slides of her river trip. They were good slides, not professional, but full of steep purple rock and shadow. Burns stood behind the couches during the presentation, eating carrot-sticks and drinking 7UP, and the Grand Canyon on the hospital wall, the foaming brown river, the two huge yellow rafts, and the travelers in their bikinis and sunglasses all gave him a kind of spin and he finally stopped eating and sat down.

"You're from Connecticut," a woman next to him said. It was Karen, the chief nurse. In the near-dark he saw that she was about his age, a brunette with an aquiline nose, like a pretty schoolteacher.

"Yes, I am," he said. The slide changed and everybody laughed: four naked people holding hands ran toward the river.

"Which one is you, Leslie?" Glen Batton said.

"Dream on, Glen," the projectionist said.

The woman next to Burns, Karen, whispered, "Before we were transferred, we lived in New London for ten years."

Lake Mead appeared as a blue plate under a pale sky. It was the first slide that had a horizontal theme and then the lights clicked on and there was applause. "This year," Leslie said to the group, "we're going to the Everglades and the Keys."

Glen Batton, who had been sitting with Julie, said, "Well, keep your clothes on around the alligators, Leslie."

"That wasn't me."

"Don't listen to him," Julie said. "He's been in Alaska too long."

People were standing up and moving the couches against the walls now, and suddenly the lights went down and a tape began to play a Beatles song that Burns knew, but didn't know the name of, and three couples began to dance. Burns went to the window and holding his hand against the pane, he saw the stars.

"The weather's clearing for a spell." One of the deputies had come up to him.

Burns looked at the man. "Did you find that dog?"

"Not today, but we will."

"How often do you have to do this."

"Not twice a year. Usually just spring. A lot of dogs are let loose. It's a bad deal."

"Come here," a man said from behind him, taking his arm. It was the counselor, the Inuit, Victor. "I'll show you something." He led Burns past Karen and down the hallway and out the side door into the cold. "Check this." The man pointed over the roof where Burns saw a finger of yellow light run up the sky and fade followed by two pale pink ones that shifted like something seen through a depth of water.

"I've never seen them before," Burns said to the man. His breath rose as white mist.

The man smiled. "Alec hadn't either," he said. "I'm sorry for what happened. He was related to you?"

"He was my son." Now a greenish white washed up the sky and flared in sections as if cooling.

"He was too smart for this place," the man said.

"What do you mean?"

"What would keep him here? All the white guys with their dog teams? Alec was a genius, right? He must be what a genius is."

"Possibly," Burns said. The cold had gone through him and become a pressure in his neck. Now the pink was back, shooting like a crazy beacon into the black.

"You're staying with Julie?"

"Yes," Burns answered, and alerted by something in Victor's voice he added, "Why?"

"Nothing," Victor said, looking up, his hands thrust deep in his pockets. "I could never figure them. Alec and her."

"I see," Burns said. For a moment the sky was black. "She's so . . ." Burns opened the sentence hoping the other man would finish it. He wanted this information.

"I don't know. I shouldn't talk. You'll see that not much up here is what it seems, but they didn't fit. She's too sociable. Maybe that's what I mean."

Suddenly a canopy of blue light came up the sky and then shredded and disappeared.

Someone took Burns's arm and he felt a body next to him. "Aren't you freezing?" Karen said. She shivered against him, hugging his arm with both hands. "It's twenty below." Burns put his arm out and around the woman.

"Do you know what happened to him?" he said to Victor.

"I don't. I took him hunting once, his first year here, before he moved out. He was good people. I never saw somebody so swept away by this place. He loved it all. He was an intense guy all around."

Karen shifted her position, running her arms around Burns's middle and burying her head in his shoulder. "It's cold!" she said, laughing. The night continued to convulse above them, a huge panorama revolving across the horizon. The sharp dry cold sized Burns's skin, his face. The food and the slides were all gone. He was awake.

"What's the weather tomorrow, Victor? Could a person fly somewhere?"

"We'll get one day," Victor said. "Tomorrow you could fly anywhere you want."

Inside, Karen kept his arm, the cold now real in the warm room. Most of the people at the party were dancing, and Burns saw Glen Batton and Julie moving slowly to the music, another song he knew but couldn't identify. He didn't know the name of five songs in the world. It was a wonder to him; he didn't know any songs.

Karen asked him if he wanted to dance and he smiled and said he had to go. She led him back to the coats, which were in the dark entry hall. She handed him his parka, and the way she looked at him, frankly, without any real pity, led him to do something he hadn't done in ten years. He leaned to her and put his free hand around her back and kissed her. She embraced him fully, but without anything frantic, and the dark of the hall and the smell of the coats made him feel like a boy again and now too he was full of resolve about tomorrow as he held her there, lifting her against him. He liked feeling her body and she shifted twice against him, moving so their legs were interwoven, and he heard her moan in the shifting coats, and he did not let go. Then he heard his name. Glen was saying his name.

"Excuse me," Glen said, coming down the dark hallway. They had disengaged by the time he spoke again. "Julie asked me to tell you that I'm willing to take you out to Kolvik tomorrow." Glen was looking at Karen. "The weather's supposed to clear."

"I appreciate that," Burns said. "Are you sure?"

"The weather is going to be splendid." Julie had come up behind him. She saw Burns putting on his coat. "Where are you going?"

"I thought I'd get some rest. Deviled eggs, the Grand Canyon, the northern lights . . . this is a lot for an old man."

"He'd never seen the lights before," Karen said, squeezing Burns's arm.

"Here," Julie said, taking his arm from Karen. "I'll go with you."

"No, please," he said. "I know the way. Please. Stay."

Julie retrieved her coat and pushed Glen back to the party. Karen stood around until she saw that Julie was serious about leaving, and then she took both of Burns's hands and reached up and kissed him quickly, drifting back to the party herself. As he opened the door for Julie and pushed out into the white night, Burns saw Batton watching them.

The night was now still, the first stillness Burns had felt in Alaska, and he felt the weight of the profound chill, the northern sky fringed with erratic blooming light. "Her husband ran the armory here," Julie said. "He was killed loading freight two years ago."

"She stayed."

Julie looked at him. "People stay," she said. "You come out, you don't go back." Julie held his arm all along the crunching snowy road and they didn't speak further, but fell into step like the oldest of friends, and Burns let the night and the cold disappear and he imagined that she was thinking what he was thinking: that tomorrow he would see where Alec died.

At Julie's trailer, the lights were on and two little boys sat at the kitchen table in their stocking feet drawing with crayons. "Well, hello, Timmo," Julie said. "How are you?" Neither boy looked up, but Burns could see their eyes looking around. "Is this your cousin?"

Timmo nodded.

"Well, good. What's he drawing?" The cousin turned

his paper a bit so Julie could see the two figures on the sheet. Burns looked at the two brown smudges. The boy traced a line from one to the other. "This is you shooting a caribou, isn't it," Julie said. "And it is very good." The boys smiled to each other. Julie opened the cupboard and put out a plate of graham crackers and poured two glasses of milk. "Now, Timmo," she said, looking at her watch, "at eleven, you must go home." She looked up at Burns. "This is Timmo and his cousin No Name." At this the boys giggled. "Timmo is an artist who comes over some nights. His mother is in the Tahoe." Burns stood there in his coat. He wanted one of the crackers. He wanted them all. He smiled at the beautiful native boys. What a day. He had been warm and cold and hungry. This was all so new.

Julie took her coat off and came over to him. "We'd better go to bed," she said. "You've got a big day ahead, and if we don't leave the room, they'll never eat the crackers."

The next afternoon, in the low white angle of sunlight, Burns walked out to Glen Batton's place, a trailer behind the Forest Service buildings. The light was terrific, knifing at Burns, and he squinted behind his sunglasses.

In the small yard he slipped and fell, and climbing awkwardly back up, saw that he had stumbled across the hindquarters of a caribou lying in the snow. "That's the freezer up here," Glen Batton said from the doorway. "Fresh meat all winter. Hop in the truck, I'll be right there."

Batton seemed in a good mood, quite happy to show Burns all he knew about the small airplane, which was tethered—along with a dozen others—out on the frozen sea. A runway had been freshly bladed through the drifts along the waterfront, and Batton talked Burns through all the preparations he made, taking off the heavy insulated blanket over the motor, checking the oil, freeing the flaps. He had Burns help him push the plane forward a foot, cracking the icy seal between the skis and the snowpack. He opened the passenger door and pointed out the emergency gear under the seat, the food, the cross-country skis, and then he pointed to a small orange box in the back of the small cargo space and said, "Don't worry about that, Mr. Burns. That will start signaling on impact."

And Glen was chatty on the way over to Kolvik, talking to Burns—over the intercom—about his work with the Forest Service. They flew up the river in the sunshine, Batton pointing out the moose and caribou. He explained that for the caribou counts he usually took one of the secretaries and that Julie didn't like that. "Did you ever have a spat with your wife, Mr. Burns?"

"A spat?"

"You know, where she's jealous over something you're doing, although you're totally innocent."

"I guess, sometimes," Burns said, his voice distant on the intercom, sounding small, like what it was: a lie. Helen had never fought with him, never complained. She had been a sweet, happy, confident woman who had—even in their extremity—never fought with him.

"Yeah, well, Julie . . ." Batton said. "That's why she left last night and went home early with you." Batton pointed ahead, where a small herd of caribou moved across the frozen river. "What am I going to do, land out there and screw Denise?"

A haze had come up, like bright smoke, and the plane rippled across the changing sky. Burns was concentrating, trying to see the country as Alec might have seen it.

"We take a lunch and stop for lunch," Glen Batton went on. "But that's lunch. People eat lunch. Right?"

The rest of the flight was different from what Burns could have foreseen. He couldn't get Glen to put down in Kolvik. They came upon the small toss of cabins which was Kolvik and Burns's heart lifted, but then it all changed quickly. There was no strip near the small village, of course, and Glen explained that it wasn't safe to land in the snow so soon after the recent storms. He made one pass by the clearing near where Alec's cabin had been and laid down a pair of tracks with the skis, but then circling he explained to Burns—through the noisy intercom—that it was too soft, too dangerous. Shoulder to shoulder with Glen Batton in the front seat of the smallest plane he'd ever been in, Burns asked again if they couldn't possibly try to land.

"No can do, Mr. Burns," Batton said, his voice tiny through the receiver, sounding miles away. "Too deep, too soft. No one else has been out either. That's where he lived"—Batton dipped the passenger wing steeply and pointed—"below that hill." There was no sign of anything in the perfect snow. They made one more broad circle over the area, seeing several moose in the valley where Alec supposedly had trapped, and then they headed west toward home. Burns felt the little plane rattle in the new headwind, the door flexing against his knee more than it had for the flight out, and he felt a disappointment that replaced hunger in his gut. He'd been so close. He could have jumped from the plane and landed in the drift. From the air, the place where his son lived had looked like all the other terrain they'd seen: snowy hills grown with small pine. Alaska gave up its stories hard. He'd learned nothing.

They had flown quite low on the way out, but now Glen was taking the plane up to three and then four thousand feet. The sun was obscured in the west in a thick roseate mist. Burns was silent, mad at first, feeling cheated, and then resolved simply on what he now knew: he would ask Blazo.

"You spoke to the sheriff," Batton said.

"I did." Even Burns's own voice sounded remote on the intercom. "He was a help."

"And now you've been to Kolvik."

"Not quite, Glen. I've flown over it."

Batton ignored him, resetting some instruments, finally saying, "Did you ever see Russia?"

"I never have."

Batton leveled the plane at five thousand feet and turned it slightly, squinting through the windshield. "You know, it's funny your being here. I wouldn't have walked across the street for my old man and here you've come all the way north to see where your kid died." Burns said nothing. "There." Glen Batton pointed at a faint solid form below the sunset. "That line. That's Russia."

Burns could see the landfall that Batton had indicated, dark and vague beneath the fading rosy dusk, and as the little aircraft was bumped and lifted, he could sense the curvature of the earth from this height. Flying into the lost light made him feel again the sorrow he'd lived by for so long. The little plane descended in rocky strokes, lurching and gliding through the darkening frigid night. The men did not speak, but when the lights of Kotzebue glimmered on the horizon, a settlement in the void, Glen Batton spoke to the airport and then said to Burns: "Look.

I know he was your son and he was a good kid, but the end was no good. He was a pain in the ass for everybody. Nearly drove Julie crazy."

Burns just listened. He wasn't mad anymore. He didn't want to argue. The lights of the village grew distinct and Batton circled out over the frozen ocean showing the town as a sweet Christmas decoration, a model, the pools of lamplight on the snowpacked streets.

"And now you're here, starting it all up again. You ought to get the flight to Anchorage tomorrow before this next weather really hits, and let Julie get on with her life."

Burns could see an orange bonfire on the hill at the edge of town and the dark forms of sleds descended the slope. Batton banked sharply, moving for the first time all day with an undue haste, and then leveled, and as the icy runway approached Burns felt the bottom drop out. The plane dipped suddenly, wrenching him up against his seat belt, where he floated for a second before slamming down. His head hit the windscreen and the edge of the console and then he felt the plane riding hard on the ridged ice, shaking him to the spine.

Batton ran the plane to the end of the runway and then wheeled it around to the tie-downs. "Sorry about that," he said. "It's always a little rough, but we hit her pretty hard that time."

Burns's hand was in the blood on his hairline and he could feel the welt rising where his forehead was split.

"You okay?" Batton asked, turning off the plane and climbing down.

"What'd you do to him, Glen? What did you do to Alec?"

With the earphones off everything sounded flat. Batton was fastening the fixed cables to each wing. Burns opened his door and jumped down onto the ice and moved

away from the plane. He was dizzy and there seemed to
be blood everywhere. Head cuts were like faucets; he'd
had plenty playing hockey.

Batton was struggling with the insulation blanket for
the engine. "You bleeding?" he said. "Let me see that."

"Were you after Julie before Alec moved?" Burns said.

Batton stopped fastening the snaps on the cover and
came around to Burns. It was clear he wanted to hit him.
The two men stood between the plane and the pickup on
the rough sea ice. "Look," Batton said. "You're a smart
guy. Julie said you went to Yale."

"Glen," Burns said, "I didn't come up here for trouble.
I came up here to see what Alec saw, something for myself.
And now I want to know what you did to him."

Glen came up to Burns and took a handful of his parka
shoulder. In the icy light, Burns could see his face, angry
and tight, and he felt himself being lifted. He didn't care.
He was bleeding. He didn't care what Glen did. Burns
saw Batton's eyes flicker over the things he was going to
do and then focus on him. "Get in," Glen said finally,
letting go of the coat. But Burns backed past the truck
and into the dark toward the mounds of ragged plate ice
between himself and the village.

Not ten minutes later, Burns found himself on a dark
side street disoriented and full of the old dread. He'd just
walked and something—the cold, the gash on his head,
the iron hardness of the packed roadway, the glimpse of
the earth growing dark—had let it all gather in his heart.
For years he had thought that the weight of it, the dark-
est part, was his drinking. He'd wake somewhere sick and
feel it around his chest like a cold hand and not be able

to swallow. But after he stopped drinking, it didn't lift. It didn't come every day, but when it came as it had tonight, it hit with a force that left him weak.

On their holidays when he and Helen would go to St. Johns, he was drunk by noon, usually, rum was such an easy thing to drink. You could drink it in anything, coffee, juice. You could drink it in milk, for chrissake. You could take warm mouthfuls right from the bottle.

You could drink vodka and bourbon from the bottle too, but not in balmy weather. In the islands it was rum. Manhattan was gin. Airplanes were gin too, the stiff chemical push in the face. Clients were scotch, something that bit and then slid in Burns, he could drink scotch for weeks. He had done it. But his rules were his rules: Manhattan was gin; St. Johns was rum; clients were scotch; and he drank vodka and bourbon those nights when the rules began to float. It was vodka the time he tried to die.

Now Burns felt the goose egg on his forehead. The blood had stopped, but the flesh was too tender to touch. He looked around and couldn't find a landmark. Four or five buildings, warehouses or churches, stood over him. He wasn't sure of the way he'd come and he couldn't tell north from south. He felt drained. He turned around searching for a clue, even a snowbank to sit on, but he could only see how much, how very much, of his own life he had missed.

Between buildings he thought he caught sight of the bonfire on the hill, and then someone took his arm. He looked down at Blazo, his grin showing the missing teeth, a man who by the wrinkles in his brown face could have been a hundred. With a firm grip on Burns's arm, Blazo marched him to the corner, out of the shadows, and pointed at the sledding fire.

"I saw them sledding," Burns said, but Blazo pointed again. A flare of powdery red light rose in the sky and then dissolved as a wave of yellow swelled and faded. "This place," Burns said. He felt dizzy. "These nights. This place is something else." He stepped away from Blazo. "Thanks," he said. "Julie's place is that way, right?"

Blazo nodded. He seemed to be examining Burns's face.

Burns started down the street and then hesitated. "I need to get to Kolvik. Soon. I need to see where Alec Burns lived, where he had a trapline. South of town."

"He was your boy," Blazo said.

Above them, the sky was relentless, the random vast armatures of colored light wheeling up and then vanishing, sometimes printing themselves from nothing on the darkness like bright stains. "He was," Burns whispered. The cold air cut at his nose as he breathed, and he could feel his pulse aching in his wound. "You can talk," Burns said.

"Not really." Blazo quickly pointed down the snow-packed lane, and Burns saw a figure trotting swiftly under the lamplight, a dog, some kind of husky, moving as with purpose. "But we'll go out there," Blazo said. "Tomorrow morning. It's going to snow, but we'll get half a day of good weather."

The trailer was dark. Burns opened the door quietly and heard a strange sound which he then recognized as the violin. He felt the warmth and it made him catch his breath. He almost wept.

As he passed through the mud room without removing his coat, he felt Molly's nose fit into his palm in the dark. His legs were trembling. Julie was playing something sharp, full of energy and angles, it filled the space completely, and Burns saw her as he passed through the living room. She sat on the ottoman in her underwear, playing by the light of two candles. He saw the shine of sweat on her forehead and breastbone, and then he was in his room, suddenly warm himself and pulling at his coat and sweater.

There was a knock at his door, and Julie was there, tying her robe. "Hi," she said. "Sorry about that. . . . What's all this blood?"

"Nothing," he said. He was sitting on the bed. "You play very well."

Julie took his chin in her hand and pulled at the cut with a thumb. "Oh, yes, it's nothing," she said. "Looks like Glen hit you with an ax."

"It was an accident," Burns said quietly. On the warm bed, with his head in a woman's hands, he felt himself letting go. Julie was standing very close. He was a serious and controlled man, and he clenched his jaw, but his eyes welled.

"I'm going to have to stitch this closed, Mr. Tom Burns, or you'll return to the East Coast with a genuine Alaskan tattoo." And in a moment she came back with a warm wet cloth and a small kit. "You want something to eat?"

"No," he said. "I'm all in." He could feel his voice unsteady. "We didn't make it. Glen couldn't land."

Burns leaned back and looked at Julie and he saw her read his face. She stood beside him and put her arm around his neck. Burns held perfectly still. "What are you doing in Alaska? I'm not so sure this is a good idea for you." She began dabbing at his forehead with the cloth.

Then Burns's head began to ache and he could feel her working at the skin with the black thread. He was pulled into the open front of her robe where freckles rose from her cleavage in warm, vertiginous constellations inches from his face and he could smell her skin and the sweet Wild Turkey on her breath. His right ear was full of dried blood and his hearing came and went. He had both of his hands on her hips and he could feel her moving against him, the warmth and pressure of her legs.

"Are you all right," Burns whispered.

He heard her say, "I know what I'm doing."

He had a high hollow feeling and his mouth tasted sweet and dry the way it did before a drunk, and Julie cinched each stitch with three short tugs and this became part of the litany, her shifting breasts, the freckles riding there, his eyes half closed in the warm room, and the steady and expected tug-tug-tug. He ran his hand inside her robe and lifted his face to kiss her. She kissed him back, pausing for a moment to move the dangling needle on its black thread out of their way. She came over onto him on the bed. "Isn't this why you've come?" Her eyes fixed him as she continued to move with each word: "Isn't it?" Burns could feel the needle riding in his ear now and Julie lifted it away. "Watch out for me. I'm not what you think."

"What do I think?"

"You think I'm some coping person. A nurse. Something. I don't even know anymore what they do in your world, but here we take comfort where we find it. Glen came after me like a dog in heat. It's like that, Tom." Julie moved against him and Burns knew she could feel that he was aroused. "I'm like that."

"No you're not," he said. Even as he heard the words, he realized he didn't know what he was saying. He'd decided who she was yesterday, standing in her kitchen. The whole journey to Alaska had seemed mad to him at first, but once he was committed, he'd decided what he would see. He had written a kind of scenario without knowing it and now it was coming undone. It was a long moment for Burns, as if he had dived into the ocean and was waiting to turn and ascend. He was airless and without will.

Julie had lifted herself and was looking into his eyes, waiting for something. She looked much older here, harder. When he didn't move, she said, "You really don't get it, do you."

"What? What is it?" he said to her. "What am I missing? Did Glen hurt Alec?"

"You're hard to believe, Tom," Julie said, rolling off him and standing by the bed. "You're too old to be that innocent." She took his head in her hands once again, but she held it differently. "Yes, Glen hurt Alec. So did I. So did this place. And probably you did too. Alec went mad. He did. But when he moved out there, Glen didn't help him. I know that. They hated each other by then, you can tell that. I knew he wouldn't land with you. I'm trying to be honest here. What happened would have happened. Glen didn't kill Alec."

"He didn't save him."

"That's what I'm telling you, Tom." Julie stood back, tugging sharply at the thread in Burns's forehead, and she looked at him frankly. "None of us did."

Burns was walking in the snow. So this is where it was, he thought. He tried to see the valley as Alec might have, and began picking his way across the meadow. The surface of the snow was crusted and his snowshoes only cut a few inches with each step. He worked into a warm rhythm of small steps up the incline, breathing into the gray afternoon. It was wonderful to move this way after being on the snow machine all day. The clouds had come down and Burns felt the air change as he marched. It lifted at him somehow, not a wind but some quickness that was sharper in his nose, and it grew darker suddenly and he saw the first petals of snow easing down around him.

At the top he turned, breathing hard, and put his hands on his hips to rest. He felt the old high thrill in his chest just like the winter days at Yale, the flasks in the stands at the rink, and crossing campus at midnight wired tight with alcohol, his coat open to the sharp tonic of the air. Now his head was almost against the somber tent of clouds and below him the snow fell as it does at sea, ponderous and invisible at once, disappearing except where it fell on his sleeves, his eyebrows. The snow was falling everywhere.

His knees burned faintly as he stepped along the crest of the hill and descended into the draw where Alec had trapped. Here the small pines were thicker and there were game trails in the snow between the clumps of trees.

The year he quit drinking, that June, he and Alec had sailed from Martha's Vineyard to the Elizabeth Islands and an exhilaration had set in that Burns remembered keenly. Alec had been on loan from Helen. They had anchored off the islands and swum the hundred yards to shore and then lain on the deserted sand, laughing and panting, and the boy had said to him, "This is it, Dad. This is the best day of my life." Burns thought at that time: I am as close to being happy as I will ever be. And he did feel happy, proud to be a good sailing coach and pleased to have captured the Elizabeth Islands on the most beautiful day in the year, but the other thing was always with him. He didn't say it before they stood and began to swim back, but Burns had decided that day to live. He would live.

Halfway up the draw, Burns stopped. This was it. He fell back in the snow, flinging out his arms. He lay there and let his heart pound him deeper. He could hear it crashing in his ears. The pin-dots of snow burned across his forehead, and his arms and legs glowed. Julie was right about Alaska: it was too warm. Burns closed his eyes. This was where Alec died. When he opened them, he stared up into the falling snow until he felt the lift of vertigo. The roaring silence was nicked by a new sound now, the snow machine buzzing closer and then—as he felt the snow fix and himself rise into the sky, weightless—a face appeared above his head.

"Right," he said to Blazo. "I'm coming. One more minute." He caught Blazo's look and added, "Don't worry. I'll get up."

"You and me," Blazo said. "We've been gone a long time already." Blazo's face disappeared, and Burns felt himself again sink into the snow. It was pleasant here, lonely and floating, and Burns stopped trying to sort his thoughts. He was hungry, and pleased to be hungry again. He could feel his feet. His blood seemed very busy. Something had a grip on him. He thought, the world has got ahold of me again. He drew a breath, the air aching in his chest, and he said, "Alec." His voice sounded sure of something. "I've been in the snow here, Alec," he said into the sky. "I've lain on my back in the snow."

II

ON THE
U. S. S. FORTITUDE

Some nights it gets lonely here on the U.S.S. Fortitude. I wipe everything down and sweep the passageways, I polish all the brass and check the turbines, and I stand up here on the bridge charting the course and watching the stars appear. This is a big ship for a single-parent family, and it's certainly better than our one small room in the Hotel Atlantis, on West Twenty-second Street. There the door wouldn't close and the window wouldn't open. Here the kids have room to move around, fresh sea air, and their own F/A-18 Hornets.

I can see Dennis now on the radar screen. He's out two hundred miles and closing, and it looks like he's with a couple of friends. I'll be able to identify them in a moment. I worry when Cherry doesn't come right home when it starts to get dark. She's only twelve. She's still out tonight, and here it is almost twenty-one hundred hours. If she's gotten vertigo or had to eject into the South China Sea, I'll just be sick. Even though it's summer, that water is cold.

There's Dennis. I can see his wing lights blinking in the distance. There are two planes with him, and I'll wait for his flyby. No sign of Cherry. I check the radar: nothing. Dennis's two friends are modified MIGs, ugly little planes that roar by like the A train, but the boys in them smile and I wave thumbs up.

These kids, they don't have any respect for the equipment. They land so hard and in such a hurry—one, two, three. Before I can get below, they've climbed out of their jets, throwing their helmets on the deck, and are going down to Dennis's quarters. "Hold it right there!" I call. It's the same old story. "Pick up your gear, boys." Dennis brings his friends over—two nice Chinese boys, who smile and bow. "Now, I'm glad you're here," I tell them. "But we do things a certain way on the U.S.S. Fortitude. I don't know what they do where you come from, but we pick up our helmets and we don't leave our aircraft scattered like that on the end of the flight deck."

"Oh, Mom," Dennis groans.

"Don't 'Oh, Mom' me," I tell him. "Cherry isn't home yet, and she needs plenty of room to land. Before you go to your quarters, park these jets below. When Cherry gets here, we'll have some chow. I've got a roast on."

I watch them drag their feet over to their planes, hop in, and begin to move them over to the elevator. It's not as if I asked him to clean the engine room. He can take care of his own aircraft. As a mother, I've learned that doing the right thing sometimes means getting cursed by your kids. It's okay by me. They can love me later. Dennis is not a bad kid; he'd just rather fly than clean up.

Cherry still isn't on the screen. I'll give her fifteen minutes and then get on the horn. I can't remember who else is out here. Two weeks ago, there was a family from Newark on the U.S.S. Tenth Amendment, but they were headed for Perth. We talked for hours on the radio, and

the skipper, a nice woman, told me how to get stubborn
skid marks off the flight deck. If you're not watching,
they can build up in a hurry and make a tarry mess.

I still hope to run across Beth, my neighbor from the
Hotel Atlantis. She was one of the first to get a carrier,
the U.S.S. Domestic Tranquillity, and she's somewhere in
the Indian Ocean. Her four girls would just be learning
to fly now. That's such a special time. We'd have so much
to talk about. I could tell her to make sure the girls always
aim for the third arresting wire, so they won't hit low or
overshoot into the drink. I'd tell her about how mad Dennis was the first time I hoisted him back up, dripping like
a puppy, after he'd come in high and skidded off the
bow. Beth and I could laugh about that—about Dennis
scowling at his dear mother as I picked him up. He was
wet and humiliated, but he knew I'd be there. A mother's
job is to be in the rescue chopper and still get the frown.

I frowned at my mother plenty. There wasn't much
time for anything else. She and Dad had a little store and
I ran orders and errands, and I mean ran—time was
important. I remember cutting through the Park, some
little bag of medicine in my hand, and watching people
at play. What a thing. I'd be taking two bottles of Pepto-
Bismol up to Ninety-first Street, cutting through the Park,
and there would be people playing tennis. I didn't have
time to stop and figure it out. My mother would be waiting back at the store with a bag of crackers and cough
medicine for me to run over to Murray Hill. But I looked.
Tennis. Four people in short pants standing inside that
fence, playing a game. Later, I read about tennis in the
paper. But tennis is a hard game to read about at first,

and it seemed a code, like so many things in my life back then, and what did it matter, anyway? I was dreaming, as my mother was happy to let me know.

But I made myself a little promise then, and I thought about it as the years passed. There was something about tennis—playing inside that fence, between those lines. I think at first I liked the idea of limits. Later, when Dennis was six or so and he started going down the block by himself, I'd watch from in front of the Atlantis, a hotel without a stoop—without an entryway or a lobby, really—and I could see him weave in and out of the sidewalk traffic for a while, and then he'd be out of sight amid the parked cars and the shopping carts and the cardboard tables of jewelry for sale. Cherry would be pulling at my hand. I had to let him go, explore on his own. But the tension in my neck wouldn't release until I'd see his red suspenders coming back. His expression then would be that of a pro, a tour guide—someone who had been around this block before.

If a person could see and understand the way one thing leads to another in this life, a person could make some plans. As it was, I'd hardly even seen the stars before, and now here, in the ocean, they lie above us in sheets. I know the names of thirty constellations, and so do my children. Sometimes I think of my life in the city, and it seems like someone else's history, someone I kind of knew but didn't understand. But these are the days: a woman gets a carrier and two kids in their Hornets and the ocean night and day, and she's got her hands full. It's a life.

And now, since we've been out here, I've been playing a little tennis with the kids. Why not? We striped a beautiful court onto the deck, and we've set up stanchions and a net. I picked up some rackets three months ago in

Madagascar, vintage T-2000s, which is what Jimmy Connors used. When the wind is calm we go out there and practice, and Cherry is getting quite good. I've developed a fair backhand, and I can keep the ball in play. Dennis hits it too hard, but what can you do—he's a growing boy. At some point, we'll come across Beth, on the Tranquillity, and maybe all of us will play tennis. With her four girls, we could have a tournament. Or maybe we'll hop over to her carrier and just visit. The kids don't know it yet, but I'm learning to fly high-performance aircraft. Sometimes when they're gone in the afternoons, I set the Fortitude into the wind at thirty knots and practice touch and go's. There is going to be something on Dennis's face when he sees his mother take off in a Hornet.

Cherry suddenly appears at the edge of the radar screen. A mother always wants her children somewhere on that screen. The radio crackles. "Mom. Mom. Come in, Mom." Your daughter's voice, always a sweet thing to hear. But I'm not going to pick up right away. She can't fly around all night and get her old mom just like that.

"Mom, on the Fortitude. Come in, Mom. This is Cherry. Over."

"Cherry, this is your mother. Over."

"Ah, don't be mad." She's out there seventy-five, a hundred miles, and she can tell I'm mad.

"Cherry, this is your mother on the Fortitude. You're grounded. Over."

"Ah, Mom! Come on. I can explain."

"Cherry, I know you couldn't see it getting dark from ten thousand feet, but I also know you're wearing your Swatch. You just get your tail over here right now. Don't bother flying by. Just come on in and stow your plane. The roast has been done an hour. I'm going below now to steam the broccoli."

Tomorrow, I'll have her start painting the superstructure. There's a lot of painting on a ship this size. That'll teach her to watch what time it is.

As I climb below, I catch a glimpse of her lights and stop to watch her land. It's typical Cherry. She makes a short, shallow turn, rather than circling and doing it right, and she comes in fast, slapping hard and screeching in the cable, leaving two yards of rubber on the deck. Kids.

I take a deep breath. It's dark now here on the U.S.S. Fortitude. The running lights glow in the sea air. The wake brims behind us. As Cherry turns to park on the elevator, I see that her starboard Sidewinder is missing. Sometimes you feel that you're wasting your breath. How many times have we gone over this? If she's old enough to fly, she's old enough to keep track of her missiles. But she's been warned, so it's okay by me. We've got plenty of paint. And, as I said, this is a big ship.

FORT BRAGG

(HOW SUBLIMINAL ADVERTISING
CHANGED MY LIFE)

It all started in my dentist's office on a day in June so beautiful that I had let my guard down, so to speak. The sun was shining in the blue sky. Birds were chirping in the trees. My L-9 molar was pounding out a pretty heavy drum solo in my skull, and so I was not my usual vigilant self. It was then I picked up a copy of *Women's Minute Magazine,* the monthly oversize glossy (which is almost all ads), and turned—by absolute accident—to page ninety-three.

I'll never forget it: the sound of the dentist's drill coming from the other room, the small acrid smell of dental smoke in the air, and my face throbbing to my splitting molar, and there on page ninety-three, a full-page photograph of the Taj Mahal at sunset. It was beautiful.

But BANG! Before I could even read the bold lettering at the bottom of the ad (I think it concerned a floor wax or a deodorant), the SUBLIMINAL MESSAGE grabbed me *in a way that would change my life forever!*

There in the reflection pond of the Taj Mahal, in points of light flashing off the dark water, were the words:

LET YOURSELF GO. LIVE IT UP! LEARN TO DANCE!

And right beneath them (and this was cleverly, slyly done in the shadow of the Taj Mahal), the unmistakable silhouette of Fred Astaire.

The next thing I knew, I was walking across the parking lot of the Floyd DeMooch Dance Studio with a big grin on my face, despite a tooth that was trying to kill me.

Inside an hour later, I had mastered the Waltz, the German Polka, the Lindy, the Stroll, the Pony, and the Southern Austrian version of the Minuet. I had really let myself go. My teacher was a lovely fragrant woman with a faint mustache. Her name was Hanna, and for a heavy woman, she was light on her feet.

I was living it up! She taught me the Tango (the dance of the year, she said) in fifteen minutes. It was during that lesson that I realized that I liked the heat of her damp face against mine and the feel of the little loaf of flesh around her waist (though I only felt it from time to time after she corrected my right-hand position on her back: thumb straight up along the spine).

Now I'm going to tell you something. During my lessons, the ad with the Taj Mahal in it et cetera softly flashed in my mind with every beat of my tooth and finally I LET MYSELF GO, as it had instructed me (see what I mean!), and I asked Hanna to marry me.

Her face beamed red under the little sheen of sweat and her mustache rose in a sweet smile that I took as the very definition of happiness!

Was I wrong!

So, we got married and it wasn't until I drove Hanna home that I had one of those realizations that men have once or twice in a lifetime: I was already married! What would I tell Doreen?

I was smart enough to sneak Hanna into the basement, an apartment she loved, and I left her there unpacking her suitcase and record player. Upstairs Doreen was on her hands and knees waxing the floor! Oh, I felt like a cad! But I decided the best thing would be to tell the truth, come clean, honesty is—after all—the best policy.

I would simply tell Doreen about the ad and how it had led me to marry someone else. Doreen was sure to understand.

I started at the beginning. A mistake. I took the ad out of my jacket pocket, where I had folded it after quietly ripping it out of the magazine in the dentist's office, and showed it to Doreen. Before I could go on about the Waltz and how the Sherbet Shuffle is just a variation on the Stroll and, incidentally, how I had married a large dance instructor who was right now humming happily in the basement, before I could explain any of it, I saw Doreen go into a kind of trance there on her hands and knees.

And then—wait until you get this!—she got up, dropped the sponge, smiled a spacey smile at me, and left the house. I couldn't figure it out. I thought perhaps she had seen me sneaking Hanna into the basement. But, no. Then I saw the answer. I stood there in the new wax which was barely dry, doing an abbreviated cha-cha-cha (it never hurts to practice), and I saw that I had inadvertently laid the ad *sideways* for Doreen and—examining it closer (cha-cha-cha)—I could see a whole other message in the reflection pond of the Taj Mahal. The ad was like one of those records you play backward to hear messages from the devil. Sideways in the reflection pond of the Taj Mahal, it said:

LIVE FAST, DIE YOUNG,
AND LEAVE A BEAUTIFUL MEMORY!

Luckily I was already on my subliminal message (cha-cha-cha) or this one would have given me a bad ride too. I ran to the window, but our old Datsun was halfway down Butternut. As the first strains of the Bossa Nova beamed up through the newly waxed floor from Hanna's record player, I thought, "There goes Doreen. I've lost my wife!"

But, as you already know, I had another.

As it turned out, I saw Doreen one more time. It was about a week later and I was awakened from an afternoon nap by what I first thought was an electrical shock, but what turned out to be my L-9 molar, which left untreated was pretty hot by now. Anyway, the television was on a weekend sports program, and I saw our Datsun zip through the screen. Well, that sat me up. It was the "Tour de l'Univers" from Budapest to Sacramento, and the cars were galloping right along. I saw the Datsun several times, and noted with rue the car's name painted across both doors: BEAUTIFUL MEMORY. In one close-up I recognized Doreen at the wheel. She had a helmet on, but I could see her smiling.

I could hear Hanna downstairs with some of her students, moving around to the music: "Come on, baby, do the twist!" And I was kind of smiling sadly about how my life had turned out, and I wasn't really watching the television commercial, which showed a house burning up while people in blankets discussed insurance.

And then: KA-BANG! In the flames I saw the message clearly, the last subliminal message before arriving here. In the bright orange of the fire danced the words:

JOIN THE ARMY

Hey, it's not so bad here at Fort Bragg. I feel a little funny, being the oldest recruit by twenty years. A lot of the kids call me *sir*. But I've organized a little group in the barracks, and I've already taught them the Hustle, the Mississippi Three Step, and the Grand Rondalay. I miss Doreen and Hanna, but I did leave Hanna the house, and I read in *Sports Illustrated* that Doreen has a good fast support team that can change a tire in seven seconds.

So, my life has changed, but who knows, the Army may help. Be all you can be, that's my motto. Boot camp is tough, but Fort Bragg is real nice. We don't have time for magazines or television, and listen: the dental care here is tremendous.

SUNNY BILLY DAY

The very first time it happened with Sunny Billy Day was in Bradenton, Florida, spring training, a thick cloudy day on the Gulf, and I was there in the old wooden bleachers, having been released only the week before after going o for 4 in Winter Park against the Red Sox, and our manager, Ketchum, saw that my troubles were not over at all. So, not wanting to go back to Texas so soon and face my family, the disappointment and my father's expectation that I'd go to work in his Allstate office, and not wanting to leave Polly alone in Florida in March, a woman who tended toward ball players, I was hanging out, feeling bad, and I was there when it happened.

My own career had been derailed by what they called "stage fright." I was scared. Not in the field—I won a Golden Glove two years in college and in my rookie year with the Pirates. I love the field, but I had a little trouble at the plate. I could hit in the cage, in fact there were times when batting practice stopped so all the guys playing pepper could come over and bet how many I was going to put in the seats. It wasn't the skill. In a game I'd walk from the on-deck circle to the batter's box and I could feel my heart go through my throat. All those people focusing on one person in the park: me. I could feel my heart drumming in my face. I was tighter than a ten-cent watch—all strikeouts and pop-ups. I went .102 for the season—the lowest official average of any starting-lineup player in the history of baseball.

Ketchum sent me to see the team psychiatrist, but that turned out to be no good, too. I saw him twice. His name was Krick and he was a small man who was losing hair, but his little office and plaid couch felt to me like the batter's box. What I'm saying is: Krick was no help—I was afraid of him, too.

Sometimes just watching others go to bat can start my heart jangling like a rock in a box, and that was how I felt that cloudy day in Bradenton as Sunny Billy Day went to the plate. We (once you play for a team, you say "we" ever after) were playing the White Sox, who were down from Sarasota, and it was a weird day, windy and dark, with those great loads of low clouds and the warm Gulf air rolling through. I mean it was a day that didn't feel like baseball.

Billy came up in the first inning, and the Chicago pitcher, a rookie named Gleason, had him 0 and 2, when the thing happened for the first time. Polly had ahold of my arm and was being extra sweet when Billy came up, to let me know that she didn't care for him at all and was with me now, but—everybody knows—when a woman acts that way it makes you nervous. The kid Gleason was a sharpshooter, a sidearm fastballer who could have struck me out with two pitches, and he had shaved Billy with two laser beams that cut the inside corner.

Gleason's third pitch was the smoking clone of the first two and Sunny Billy Day, my old friend, my former roommate, lifted his elbows off the table just like he had done twice before and took the third strike.

It *was* a strike. We all knew this. We'd seen the two previous pitches and everybody who was paying attention knew that Gleason had nailed Billy to the barn door. There was no question. Eldon Finney was behind the plate, a major league veteran, who was known as Yank because of the way he yanked a fistful of air to indicate a strike. His gesture was unmistakable, and on that dark day last March, I did not mistake it. But as soon as the ump straightened up, Sunny Billy, my old teammate, and the most promising rookie the Pirates had seen for thirty years, tapped his cleats one more time and stayed in the box.

"What's the big jerk doing?" Polly asked me. You hate to hear a girl use a phrase like that, "big jerk," when she could have said something like "rotten bastard," but when you're in the stands, instead of running wind sprints in the outfield, you take what you can get.

On the mound in Bradenton, Gleason was confused. Then I saw Billy shrug at the ump in a move I'd seen a hundred times as roommates when he was accused of *anything* or asked to pay his share of the check at the Castaway. A dust devil skated around the home dugout and out to first, carrying an ugly litter of old sno-cone papers and cigarette butts in its brown vortex, but when the wind died down and play resumed, there was Sunny Billy Day standing in the box. I checked the scoreboard and watched the count shift to 1 and 2.

Eldon "the Yank" Finney had changed his call.

So that was the beginning, and as I said, only a few people saw it and knew this season was going to be a little different. Billy and I weren't speaking—I mean, Polly was with me now, and so I couldn't ask him what was up—

but I ran into Ketchum at the Castaway that night and he came over to our table. Polly had wanted to go back there for dinner—for old times' sake; it was in the Castaway where we'd met one year ago. She was having dinner with Billy that night, the Bushel o' Shrimp, and they asked me to join them. Billy had a lot of girls and he was always good about introducing them around. Come on, a guy like Billy had nothing to worry about from other guys, especially me. He could light up a whole room, no kidding, and by the end of an hour there'd be ten people sitting at his table and every chair in the room would be turned his way. He was a guy, and anybody will back me up on this, who had the magic.

Billy loved the Castaway. "This is exotic," he'd say. "Right? Is this a South Sea island or what?" And he meant it. You had to love him. Some dim dive pins an old fishing net on the wall and he'd be in paradise.

Anyway, Polly had ordered the Bushel o' Shrimp again and we were having a couple of Mutineers, the daiquiri deal that comes in a skull, when Ketchum came over and asked me—as he does every time we meet—"How you feeling, kid?" which means have I still got the crippling heebie-jeebies. He has told me all winter that if I want another shot, just say so. Well, who doesn't want another shot? In baseball—no matter what you hear—there are no ex-players, just guys waiting for the right moment for a comeback.

I told Ketchum that if anything changed, he'd be the first to know. Then I asked him what he thought of today's game and he said, "The White Sox are young."

"Yeah," I said. "Especially that pitcher."

"I wouldn't make too much out of that mix-up at the plate today. You know Billy. He's a kind that can change the weather." Ketchum was referring to the gray pre-season game a year before. Billy came up in a light rain when a slice of sunlight opened on the field like a beacon, just long enough for everyone to see my roommate golf a low fastball into the right-field seats for a round trip. It was the at-bat that clinched his place on the roster, and that gave him his nickname.

"Billy Day is a guy who gets the breaks." Ketchum reached into the wicker bushel and sampled one of Polly's shrimp. "And you know what they say about guys who get a lot of breaks." Here he gave Polly a quick look. "They keep getting them." He stood up and started to walk off. "Call me if you want to hit a few. We don't head north until April Fools' Day."

"I don't like that guy," Polly said when he'd left. "I never liked him." She pushed her load of shrimp away. "Let's go." I was going to defend the coach there, a guy who was fair with his men and kept the signals (steal, take, hit-and-run) simple, but the evening had gone a little flat for me too. There we were out to celebrate, but as always the room was full of Billy Day. He was everywhere. He was in the car on the way back to the hotel; he was in the elevator; he was in the room; and—if you want to know it—he was in the bed too. I knew that he was in Polly's dreams and there he was in my head, turning back to the umpire, changing a strike to a ball.

The papers got ahold of what was going on during the last week of March. It was a home game against the Yankees and it was the kind of day that if there were no base-ball, you'd invent it to go with the weather. The old Bradenton stands were packed and the whole place smelled of popcorn and coconut oil. Polly was wearing a yellow sundress covered with black polka dots, the kind of dress you wear in a crowded ballpark if you might want one of the players to pick you out while he played first. By this time I was writing a friendly little column for the *Pittsburgh Dispatch* twice a week on "Lifestyles at Spring Training," but I had not done much with Billy. He was getting plenty of legitimate ink, and besides—as I said—we weren't really talking. I liked the writing, even though this was a weird time all around. I kind of *had* to do it, just so I felt useful. I wasn't ready to go home.

It was a good game, two-two in the ninth. Then Billy made a mistake. With one down, he had walked and stolen second. That's a wonderful feeling being on second with one out. There's all that room and you can lead the extra two yards and generally you feel pretty free and cocky out there. I could see Billy was enjoying this feeling, leaving cleat marks in the clay, when they threw him out. The pitcher flipped the ball backhand to the shortstop, and they tagged Billy. Ralph "the Hammer" Fox was umping out there, and he jumped onto one knee in his famous out gesture and wheeled his arm around and he brought the hammer down: OUT! After the tag, Billy stood up and went over and planted both feet on the base.

"What?" Polly took my arm.

Ralph Fox went over and I could see Billy smiling while he spoke. He patted Ralph's shoulder. Then Fox turned and gave the arms-out gesture for safe—twice—and hollered, "Play ball." It was strange, the kind of thing that makes you sure you're going to get an explanation later.

But the ballpark changed in a way I was to see twenty times during the season: a low quiet descended, not a silence, but an eerie even sound like two thousand people talking to themselves. And the field, too, was stunned, the players standing straight up, their gloves hanging down like their open mouths during the next pitch, which like everything else was now half-speed, a high hanging curve which Red Sorrows blasted over the scoreboard to win the game.

Well, it was no way to win a ballgame, but that wasn't exactly what the papers would say. Ralph Fox, of course, wasn't speaking to the press (none of the umpires would), and smiling Sunny Billy Day only said one thing that went out on the wire from coast to coast: "Hey guys, come on. You saw that Mickey Mouse move. I was safe." Most writers looked the other way, noting the magnitude of Red Sorrows's homer, a "towering blast," and going on to speculate whether the hit signaled Sorrows's return from a two-year slump. So, the writers avoided it, and in a way I understand. Now I have become a kind of sportswriter and I know it is not always easy to say what you mean. Sometimes if the truth is hard, typing it can hurt again.

There were so many moments that summer when some poor ump would stand in the glare of Billy's smile and toe the dirt, adjust his cap, and change the call. Most of the scenes were blips, glitches: a last swing called a foul ticker; a close play called Billy's way; but some were big, bad, and ugly—so blatant that they had the fans looking at their shoes. Billy had poor judgment. In fact, as I think about it, he had no judgment at all. He was a guy with the gift who had spent his whole life going forward from one thing to the next. People liked him and things came his way. When you first met Billy, it clicked: who is this guy? Why do I want to talk to him? Ketchum assigned us to room together and in a season of hotel rooms, I found out that it had always been that way for him. He had come out of college with a major in American Studies, and he could not name a single president. "My teachers liked me," he said. "Everybody likes me."

He had that right. But he had no judgment. I'd seen him with women. They'd come along, one, two, three, and he'd take them as they came. He didn't have to choose. If he'd had any judgment, he never would have let any woman sit between him and Polly.

Oh, that season I saw him ground to short and get thrown out at first. He'd trot past, look back, and head for the dugout, taking it, but you got the impression it was simply easier to keep on going than stop to change the call. And those times he took it, lying there a foot from third dead out and then trotting off the field, or taking the third strike and then turning for the dugout, you could feel the waves of gratitude from the stands. Those times I know you could feel it, because there weren't many times when Billy Day took it, and as the season wore on, and the Pirates rose to first place, they became increasingly rare.

Sunny Billy Day made the All-Stars, of course. He played a fair first base and he was the guy you couldn't get out. But he was put on the five-day disabled list, "to rest a hamstring," the release said. But I think it was Ketchum being cagey. He wasn't going to gain anything by having a kid who was developing a reputation for spoiling ball games go in and ruin a nice July night in Fenway for fans of both leagues.

By August, it was all out: Billy Day could have his way. You never saw so much written about the state of umping. Billy was being walked most of the time now. Every once in a while some pitcher would throw to him, just to test the water. They were thinking Ketchum was going to pull the plug, tell Billy to face the music, to swallow it if he went down swinging, but it never happened. The best anybody got out of it was a flyout, Billy never contested a flyout. And Ketchum, who had thirty-four good years in the majors and the good reputation to go with them, didn't care. A good reputation is one thing; not having been in the Series is another. He would be seventy by Christmas and he wanted to win it all once, even if it meant letting Billy have his way. Ketchum, it was written, had lost his judgment too.

I was writing my head off, learning how to do it and liking it a little more. It's something that requires a certain amount of care and it is done alone at a typewriter, not in the batting box in front of forty thousand citizens. And I found I was a hell of a typist; I liked typing. But I wasn't typing about my old roommate—at all. I missed him though, don't think I didn't miss him. I had plenty to say about the rest of the squad, how winning became them, made them into men after so many seasons of having to have their excuses ready before they took the field. Old Red Sorrows was hitting .390 and hadn't said the word "retirement" or the phrase "next season" in months. There was a lot to write about without dealing with Billy Day's behavior.

But, as September came along, I was getting a lot of pressure for interviews. I had been his roommate, hadn't I? What was he like? What happened to my career? Would I be back? Wasn't I dating Billy Day's girl? I soft-pedaled all this, saying "on the other hand" fifty times a week, and that's no good for athletes or writers. On the topic of Polly I said that we were friends. What a word. The papers went away and came out with what they'd wanted to say anyway: that Billy Day's old roommate had stolen his girl and now he wouldn't write about him. They used an old file photograph of Billy and Polly in the Castaway and one of Billy and me leaning against the backstop in Pittsburgh, last year, the one year I played in the major leagues. Our caps are cocked back, and we are smiling.

During all this, Polly stopped coming to the games with me. She'd had enough of the Pirates for a while, she said, and she took a job as a travel agent and got real busy. We were having, according to the papers, "a relationship," and that term is fine with me, because I don't know what else to say. I was happy to have such a pretty girl to associate with, but I knew that her real ambition was to be with Billy Day.

The Pirates won their division by twenty-eight games, a record, and then they took the National League pennant by whipping the Cardinals four straight. With Billy talking the umps into anything he wanted, and the rest of the team back from the dead and flying in formation, the Pirates were a juggernaut.

It took the Indians seven games to quiet the Twins, and the Series was set. Pirate October, they called it.

The Cleveland Press was ready for Billy. They'd given him more column inches than the Indians total in those last weeks, cataloguing his "blatant disregard for the rules and the dignity of fair play." Some of those guys could write. Billy had pulled one stunt in the playoffs that really drew fire. In game four, with the Pirates ahead five-zip, he bunted foul on a third strike and smiled his way out of it.

As one writer put it, "We don't put up with that kind of thing in Cleveland. We don't like it and we don't need it. When we see disease, we inoculate." As I said, these guys, some of them, could write. Their form of inoculation was an approved cadre of foreign umpires. They brought in ten guys for the Series. They were from Iceland, Zambia, England, Ireland, Hungary, Japan (three), Venezuela, and Tonga. When they met the press, they struck me as the most serious group of men I'd ever seen assembled. It looked good: they knew the rules and they were grim. And the Tongan, who would be behind the plate for game one, looked fully capable of handling anything that could come up with one hand.

Polly didn't go out to Cleveland with me. She had booked a cruise, a month, through the Panama Canal and on to the islands far across the Pacific Ocean, and she was going along as liaison. She smiled when she left and kissed me sweetly, which is just what you don't want your girl to do. She kissed me like I was a writer.

So I went out alone and stayed in the old Hotel Barnard, where a lot of the writers stay. It was lonely out there in Ohio, and I thought about it. It was the end of a full season in which I had not played ball, and here I was in a hotel full of writers, which I had become, instead of over at the Hilton with my club.

I was closing down the bar the night before the Series opener when Billy Day walked in. I couldn't believe my eyes.

"I thought I'd find you here," he said.

"Billy," I said, waving the barman to bring down a couple of lagers. "I'm a writer now. This is where the writers stay. You're out after curfew."

He gestured back at the empty room. "Who's gonna write me up, you?" He smiled his terrific smile and I realized as much as I had avoided him for eight months, I missed him. I missed that smile.

"No," I said. "I don't think so." Our beers came and I asked him, "What's up?"

"It's been a rough season."

"Not from what I read. The Pirates won the pennant."

"Jesus," he said. "What is that, sarcasm? You gonna start talking like a writer too?"

"Billy, you've pulled some stunts."

He slid his beer from one hand to the other on the varnished bar of the Hotel Barnard. And then started to nod. "Yeah," he said. "I guess I did. You know, I didn't see it at first. It just kind of grew."

"And now you know."

"Yeah, now I know all about it. I know what I can do."

"So what brings you out on a night to the Hotel Barnard?" I pointed at his full glass of beer. "It's not the beer."

"You," he said, and he turned to me again and smiled. "You always knew what to do. I don't mean on the field. There was no rookie better. But I mean, what should I do? This is the Series."

"Yeah, it's the Series. If I were you, I'd play ball."

"You know what I mean. Ketchum wants me to use it all. He doesn't care if they tear down the stadium."

"And you?"

"I don't know. All my life, I played to win. It seems wrong not to do something that can help your team. But the people don't like it."

I looked at the clouds crossing the face of Sunny Billy Day, and I knew I was seeing something no man had ever seen there before: second thoughts.

"These new umps may not let you get away with anything."

"Kid," he said to me, touching my shoulder with his

fist, his smile as wide and bright as the sun through a pop-up, "I've been missing you. But I thought you knew me better than that. I've lived my life knowing one thing: everybody lets me get away with everything. The only thing I ever lost, I lost to you. Polly. And I didn't even think about it until she was gone. How is she?"

"I'd get her back for you if I could," I said, lifting my glass in a toast to my old friend Billy Day. "Polly," I told him, "is headed for Tahiti."

Billy was right about the umps. They looked good, in fact, when they took the field and stood with their arms behind their backs along the first-base line, they looked like the Supreme Court. The people of Cleveland were ready for something too, because I noted in the article I wrote for the *Dispatch* that the squadron of umpires received a louder ovation when they took the field than the home team did. Everybody knew that without an iron heel from the umps, the Indians might as well take the winter off.

Okay, so it was baseball for several innings. Ohio in October smells sweet and old, and for a while I think we were all transported through the beautiful fall day, the stadium bathing in the yellow light and then pitching steeply into the sepia shadow of the upper decks. See: I was learning to write like the other guys.

Sunny Billy Day hadn't been a factor, really, walking twice and grounding a base hit into left. It was just base-ball, the score two to one Cleveland in the top of the eighth. Now, I want to explain what happened carefully. There were seventy-four thousand people there and in the days since the Series I've heard almost that many versions. The thirty major papers disagreed in detail and the video-tapes haven't got it all because of the angle and sequence. So let me go slow here. After all, it would be the last play of Sunny Billy Day.

I wasn't in the press box. The truth is that the season had been a little hard on me in terms of making friends with my fellow reporters. I'd had a hundred suppers in half-lit lounges and I don't think it came as a surprise that I didn't really care for the way they talked—not just about baseball, for which they had a curious but abiding dis-dain. And I'm not one of these guys who think you have to have played a sport—or really done anything—to be able to write about it well. Look at me—I was good in the field, but I can't write half as good as any of the guys I travel with. But sportswriters, when they are together at the end of the day, a group of them having drinks wait-ing for their Reuben sandwiches to arrive, are a fairly superior and hard-bitten bunch. You don't want to wan-der into one of these hotel lounges any summer evening if you want to hear anything about the joy of the sport. These guys don't celebrate baseball, and really, like me, they don't analyze it very well. But they have *feelings* about it; I never met a man who didn't. That's why it's called the major leagues.

Anyway, I don't want to get going on writers and all that stuff. And don't get me wrong. Some of them—hell, most of them—are nice guys and quick about the check or asking how's it going, but it was October and it was all getting to me. I could see myself in two years, flipping my ash into somebody's coffee cup offering a weary expert's opinion. So I wanted to sit where someone might actually cheer or spill a little beer when they stood up on a third strike or a home run. Journalists are professionals, anyone will tell you this, and they don't spill their beer. I ended up ten rows behind third in a seat I paid for myself, and it turned out to be a lucky break given what was going to happen.

With one out in the top of the eighth, Billy Day doubled to right. It was a low fastball and he sliced it into the corner.

On the first pitch to Red Sorrows, Coach Ketchum had Billy steal. He's one run down with one out in the eighth, a runner in scoring position, and a fair hitter at the plate, and Ketchum flashes the steal sign—it's crazy. It means one thing: he's trading on Billy's magic all the way. When I saw Ketchum pinch his nose and then go to the bill of his cap, which has been the Pirate's steal sign for four years, I thought: Ketchum's going to use Billy any way he can. The pitch is a high strike which Sorrows fouls straight back against the screen, so now everybody knows. Billy walks back to second. I have trouble believing what I see next. Again Ketchum goes to his nose and his cap: steal. The Cleveland hurler, the old veteran Blade Medina, stretches and whirls to throw to second with Billy caught halfway down and throws the ball into center field. He must have been excited. Billy pulls into third standing.

Okay, I thought, Ketchum, you got what you wanted, now *stop screwing around*. In fact, I must have whispered that or said it aloud, because the guy next to me says to my face, "What'd I do?" These new fans. They don't want to fight you anymore, they want to know how they've offended you. Too much college for this country. I told him I was speaking to someone else, and he let it go, until I felt a tap on my shoulder and he'd bought me a beer. What did I tell you? But I didn't mind. A minute later I would need it.

Sorrow goes down swinging. Two outs.

It was then I got a funny feeling, on top of all the other funny feelings I'd been having in the strangest summer of my life, and it was a feeling about Ketchum, and I came to know as I sipped my beer and watched my old coach walk over to Billy on the bag at third that he was going to try to steal home. Coach Ketchum was the king of the fair shake, a guy known from Candlestick to Fenway as a square shooter, and as he patted Billy on the rump and walked back to the coach's box, I saw his grin. I was ten rows up and the bill of his cap was down, but I saw it clearly—the grin of a deranged miser about to make another two bucks.

Billy had never stolen home in his career.

Blade Medina was a tall guy and as he launched into his windup, kicking his long leg toward third, Billy took off. Billy Day was stealing home; you could feel every mouth in the stadium open. Blade Medina certainly opened his. Then he simply cocked and threw to the catcher, who tagged Billy out before he could decide to slide.

Ketchum was on them before the big Tongan umpire could put his thumb away. For a big guy he had a funny out call, flicking his thumb as if shooting a marble. I have to hand it to Billy. He was headed for the dugout. But Ketchum got him by the shirt and dragged back out to the plate and made him speak to the umpire. You knew it was going to happen again—and in the World Series—because all the Indians just stood where they were on the field. And sure enough after a moment of Ketchum pushing Billy from the back, as if he was some big puppet in a baseball suit, and Billy speaking softly to the umpire, the large official stepped out in front of the plate and swept his hand out flat in the air as if calming the waters: "Safe!" he said. He said it quietly in his deep voice. Well, it was quiet in Cleveland, do you see? I sat there like everyone else looking at the bottom of my plastic glass of beer and wishing it wasn't so. Seventy-four thousand people sitting in a circle feeling sour in their hearts, not to mention all the sad multitudes watching the televised broadcast.

Then my old coach Ketchum made it worse by hauling Billy over to touch the plate; Billy hadn't even stepped on home base yet. Just typing this makes me feel the ugliness all over again.

But then the real stuff started to happen, and, as I said, there were no good reports of this next part because of everybody looking at their shoes, programs, or their knuckles the way people in a restaurant read the menu real hard when a couple is arguing at the next table. But I saw it, and it redeemed Sunny Billy Day forever to me, and it gave me something that has allowed me, made me really, get out my cleats again and become a baseball player. I'm not so bad a writer that I would call it courage, but it was definitely some big kick in the ass.

What happened was, halfway back to the dugout, *Billy turned around*. His head was down in what I called *shame* in my report to the *Pittsburgh Dispatch,* and he turned around and went back to home plate. Ketchum was back at third, smug as a jewel thief, and he caught the action too late to do anything about it. Billy took the ump by the sleeve and I saw Billy take off his cap and shake his head and point at the plate. We all knew what he was saying, everybody. The ballpark was back, everyone standing now, watching, and we all saw the big Tongan nod and smile that big smile at Ketchum, and then raise his fist and flick his thumb.

Oh god, the cheer. The cheer went up my spine like a chiropractor. There was joy in Ohio and it went out in waves around the world. I wrote that too. Not joy at the out; joy at order restored. It was the greatest noise I've ever heard. I hope Billy recognized the sound.

Because what happened next, as the Cleveland Indians ran off the field like kids, and Ketchum's mouth dropped open like the old man he would become in two minutes, surprised everyone, even me.

When the Pirates took the field (and they ran out joyfully too—it was baseball again), there was something wrong. The Pirates pitcher threw his eight warm-up pitches and one of the Cleveland players stepped into the box. That is when the Irishman umping first came skittering onto the field wheeling his arms, stopping play before it had begun, and seventy-four thousand people looked over to where I'd been staring for five minutes: first base. There was no one at first base. Sunny Billy Day had not taken the field.

I wish to this day I'd been closer to the field because I would have hopped the rail and run through the dugout to the clubhouse and found what the batboy said he found: Billy's uniform hung in his locker, still swinging on the hanger. I asked him later if he got a glimpse of a woman in a yellow dress, but he couldn't recall.

And now, this spring, I'm out again. I'd almost forgotten during my long season in the stands how much fun it was to play baseball. I still have a little trouble at the plate and I ride my heartbeat like a cowboy on a bad bull, but I want to play, and if I remember that and hum to myself a little while I'm in the box, it helps. The new manager is a good guy and if I can keep above .200, he'll start me.

Oh, the Indians won the series, but it went six games and wasn't as one-sided as you might think after such an event. Ketchum stayed in the dugout the whole time, under heavy sedation, though I never mentioned that in my stories. And I never mentioned the postcards I got later from the far island of Pago Pago. I still get them. Sometimes I'll carry one in my pocket when I go to the plate. It's a blue-and-green place mainly, and looks like a great place for a lucky guy and a woman who looks good in summer clothing.

Sunny Billy Day was a guy with a gift. You could see it a mile away. Things came his way. Me, I'm going to have to make my own breaks, but, hey, it's spring again and it feels like life is opening up. I'm a lot less nervous at the plate these days, and I have learned to type.

THE TABLECLOTH
OF TURIN

A man, anywhere from forty to sixty, comes onto the stage. He wears glasses, a white shirt with the sleeves rolled up, wool slacks, and shined black shoes. Under his arm he carries a folded tablecloth. It is very large. He is also carrying a folding desk lamp, a pointer, and a packet of other small gear. The man, Leonard Christofferson, pins the tablecloth to the backdrop, sets up the desk lamp to illuminate the tablecloth, lifts the pointer, and steps toward the audience.

This is the seventy-first public appearance of the famed Tablecloth of Turin. My name is Leonard Christofferson, and the tablecloth and I have been traveling for almost three months now. I am an insurance investigator by trade from Ann Arbor, Michigan, but I've pretty much let that all go. After all, it is my tablecloth, and it is my wish to share it and show it to as many folks as I can.

In the last three months, I've met with a lot of skepticism about the authenticity of the cloth, but most people—when they hear the story and see the evidence—come to know as well as I do that this is the tablecloth of the Last Supper, the very cloth depicted in so many famous paintings, including Leonardo da Vinci's, the very tablecloth over which Christ broke that bread and poured that wine.

I want to say right here: as an insurance investigator, I had many years experience with and exposure to frauds, some of them silly, some of them so well constructed as to seem genuine. We had homicides made to look like drunk driving and a bad curve; we had grand larcenies perpetrated by nephews, nieces, wives, and sons, all in cahoots with the "victim"; we had an insured Learjet go down to the bottom of Lake Michigan which upon salvage turned out to be a junked boxcar, the jet having been sold in Mexico. In my experience as a detective, I learned slowly over the years to trust nothing, nobody. It's a terrible profession, picking through death cars and the ashes of every dry cleaner's that burns up. The owner stands there hating you and you don't trust him, a guy you never met before in your life. The twelve years I worked for Specific Claims in Ann Arbor were hard years on me, and they destroyed my faith in the human race.

And when I went to Italy with the Art Guild and I found, well, I was offered, this piece of white cloth, I saw my chance to turn my life around. I do not now speak nor have I ever spoken Italian, but I could see from the ardor in the man's eyes that he too had recovered his faith and he wanted me to take care of this sacred emblem in a way that he, working in his brother's restaurant, could never do. I paid him, left the Art Guild Renaissance trip early, flew back to Ann Arbor, and quit my job, and I have been sharing my good fortune ever since.

Enough about me. Let me show you my tablecloth.

As you can see, it's a large one: six foot five by twenty-three feet. We have had it all chemically analyzed and I want to share our findings with you tonight. The cloth itself is one piece, constructed of rough linen, approximately fourteen threads per inch, woven on a hand loom in about, we estimate, twenty-nine A.D. X-rays have revealed thirteen place settings, most of them three-piece settings of an iron clay material, which means there were over forty dishes on the table and possibly fifty, depending on how many carafes of wine were out.

This is where Christ sat. We know this not only from historical and artistic record, but also from the fact that this one space, this seat of honor, is unmarked. Under the spectrometer all the other places have revealed breadcrumbs, spilled wine, palm prints (the oil of the human hand), in one place elbow prints (someone, possibly James the Lesser, had his sleeves rolled up), but Christ's place is clean. He not only was a careful eater, he probably didn't have that much to eat, knowing what he knew.

Examination has also revealed some shocking new evidence: *the apostles didn't all sit on one side of the table.* Three of the places, including the place where Judas Iscariot sat, were opposite Jesus. So: sorry, Leonardo, thanks for giving us all their faces, but the truth has three backs to the camera. We suspect that Judas sat opposite Jesus for the reasons that science has supplied. In fact, science, the ultimate detective, has unraveled the whole story of the Last Supper from this humble tablecloth.

Listen: *it was a nervous dinner.* We know this from the number of wineglass rings in the cloth itself. The men were picking up their glasses and setting them down more · frequently than simply for drinking. They were playing with their glasses as if they were chess pieces.

These people would have been nervous for a number of reasons. None of the thirteen men in that room (with the possible exception of Jesus, who somehow knew the host) had ever eaten there before. Imagine it, you go to a new city, find a man carrying a pitcher of water down the street as Jesus had instructed you, and *ask him to have you* to Passover Dinner. It's an upstairs room with a limited view. Your host, whoever he is, doesn't eat with you. It is a strange setup. So, you're nervous. You sit there. You'd tap your glass too, maybe as many as seventy times, like Andrew, who sat here, did.

Then during dinner, your leader starts in on some topics which any one of us might think inappropriate for the supper table. Instead of the usual reaffirming and pleasant messages, the conversation is full of hostile assertions, statements of doom and gloom. Jesus says, "Verily I say unto you, that one of you shall betray me." Try that at home sometime, see if somebody doesn't spill the wine. Which, our spectrometer shows, every one of the twelve disciples did, the largest spill being here, where Judas sat. In addition, traces of breadcrumbs were found here, as we found everywhere, but these were partially decomposed via the starch-splitting enzymes found in human saliva, so we know almost certainly that Mr. Iscariot, almost two thousand years before the Heimlich Maneuver, choked on his bread when Jesus said that. We don't know who patted him on the back.

There is another large spill here (thirty-six square centimeters), and we theorize that Peter was still sitting when Jesus told him he would deny Jesus thrice before dawn.

From the shape of the spill, something like a banana, it seems that Peter stood to protest, and dragged his glass with him.

Other evidence in this sacred cloth suggests that besides bread and wine, the attendees at the Last Supper enjoyed a light salad with rich vinegar and some kind of noodle dish. There was no fish. The wine was a seasoned, full-bodied red wine, which our analysis has revealed to be a California wine. This last bit of evidence has given the skeptics great joy, but I've got news for you. That it is a California wine does not mean that this is not the Table-cloth of Turin; it simply means that civilization in California is older than some people now think.

When I look at this magnificent cloth and see its amazing tale of love and faith and betrayal written for all to see in wine, bread, and prints of human hands, I'm suddenly made glad again that I went to Turin last fall with the Art Guild, that I met Antony Cuppolini in his brother's restaurant, and that for some strange reason known only to God, Antony made me caretaker of this, the beautiful Tablecloth of Turin.

A KIND OF FLYING

By our wedding day, Brady had heard the word *luck* two hundred times. Everybody had advice, especially her sister Linda, who claimed to be "wise to me." Linda had wisdom. She was two years older and had wisely married a serviceman, Butch Kistleburg, whose status as a GI in the army guaranteed them a life of travel and adventure. They were going to see the world. If Brady married me, Linda told everybody, she would see nothing but the inside of my carpet store.

Linda didn't like my plans for the ceremony. She thought that letting my best man, Bobby Thorson, sing "El Paso" was a diabolical mistake. " 'El Paso,' " she said. "Why would you sing that at a wedding in Stevens Point, Wisconsin?" I told her: because I liked the song, I'm a sucker for a story, and because it was a love song, and because there *wasn't* a song called "Stevens Point."

"Well," she said that day so long ago, "that is no way to wedded bliss."

I wasn't used to thinking of things in terms of bliss, and I had no response for her. I had been thinking of the great phrase from the song that goes ". . . maybe tomorrow a bullet may find me . . ." and I was once again recommitted to the musical part of the program.

What raised *all* the stakes was what Brady did with the cake. She was a photographer even then and had had a show that spring in the Stevens Point Art Barn, a hilarious series of eye-tricks that everyone thought were double exposures: toy soldiers patrolling bathroom sinks and cowboys in refrigerators. Her family was pleased by what they saw as a useful hobby, but the exhibition of photographs had generally confused them.

When Brady picked up the wedding cake the morning we were wed, it stunned her, just the size of it made her grab her camera. She and Linda had taken Clover Lane, by the Gee place, and Brady pictured it all: the cake in the foreground and the church in the background, side by side.

When Brady pulled over near the cottonwoods a quarter mile from the church, Linda was not amused. She stayed in the car. Brady set the wedding cake in the middle of the road, backed up forty feet, lay down on the hardtop there, and in the rangefinder she saw the image she wanted: the bride and the groom on top of the three-tiered cake looking like they were about to step over onto the roof of the First Congregational Church. We still have the photograph. And when you see it, you always hear the next part of the story.

Linda screamed. Brady, her eye to the viewfinder, thought a truck was coming, that she was a second away from being run over on her wedding day. But it wasn't a truck. Linda had screamed at two birds. Two crows, who had been browsing the fenceline, wheeled down and fell upon the cake, amazed to find the sweetest thing in the history of Clover Lane, and before Brady could run forward and prevent it, she saw the groom plucked from his footing, ankle deep in frosting, and rise—in the beak of the shiny black bird—up into the June-blue sky.

"Man oh man oh man," Linda said that day to Brady. "That is a bad deal. "That," she said, squinting at the two crows, who were drifting across Old Man Gee's alfalfa, one of them with the groom in his beak, "is a definite message." Then Linda, who had no surplus affection for me, went on to say several other things which Brady has been good enough, all these years, to keep to herself.

When Bobby Thorson and I reached the church, Linda came out as we were unloading his guitar and said smugly, "Glen, we're missing the groom."

Someone called the bakery, but it was too late for a replacement, almost one o'clock. I dug through Brady's car and found some of her guys: an Indian from Fort Apache with his hatchet raised in a nonmatrimonial gesture; the Mummy, a translucent yellow; a kneeling green soldier, his eye to his rifle; and a little blue frogman with movable arms and legs. I was getting married in fifteen minutes.

The ceremony was rich. Linda read some Emily Dickinson; my brother read some Robert Service; and then Bobby Thorson sang "El Paso," a song about the intensities of love and a song which seemed to bewilder much of the congregation.

When Brady came up the aisle on her father's arm, she looked like an angel, her face blanched by seriousness and—I found out later—fear of evil omens. At the altar she whispered to me, "Do you believe in symbols?" Thinking she was referring to the rings, I said, "Of course, more than ever!" Her face nearly broke. I can still see her mouth quiver.

Linda didn't let up. During the reception when we were cutting the cake, Brady lifted the frogman from the top and Linda grabbed her hand: "Don't you ever lick frosting from any man's feet."

I wanted to say, "They're flippers, Linda," but I held my tongue.

That was twenty years ago this week. So much has happened. I've spent a thousand hours on my knees carpeting the rooms and halls and stairways of Stevens Point. Brady and I now have three boys who are good boys, but who—I expect—will not go into the carpet business. Brady has worked hard at her art. She is finished with her new book, *Obelisks,* which took her around the world twice photographing monuments. She's a wry woman with a sense of humor as long as a country road. Though she's done the traveling and I've stayed at home, whenever she sees any bird winging away, she says to me: *There you go.*

And she may be kind of right with that one. There have been times when I've ached to drop it all and fly away with Brady. I've cursed the sound of airplanes overhead and then when she comes home with her camera case and dirty laundry, I've flown to her—and she to me. You find out day after day in a good life that your family is the journey.

And now Linda's oldest, Trina, is getting married. We're having a big family party here in Stevens Point. Butch and Linda have all come north for a couple of weeks. Butch has done well; he's a lieutenant colonel. He's stationed at Fort Bliss and they all seem to like El Paso.

Trina came into the store yesterday pretending to look at carpet. People find out you're married for twenty years, they ask advice. What would I know? I'm just her uncle and I've done what I could. For years I laid carpet so my wife could be a photographer, and now she'll be a photographer so I can retire and coach baseball. Life lies before us like some new thing.

It's quiet in the store today. I can count sparrows on the wire across the road. My advice! She smiled yesterday when I told her. Just get married. Have a friend sing your favorite song at the wedding. Marriage, she said, what is it? Well, I said, it's not life on a cake. It's a bird taking your head in his beak and you walk the sky. It's marriage. Sometimes it pinches like a bird's mouth, but it's definitely flying, it's definitely a kind of flying.

III

THE GOLF CENTER
AT TEN-ACRES

I'm sitting in a lawn chair in the shade of our house, spraying the kids as they run across the front lawn. We've clothespinned an old bedspread and a tarp over the swing set, and the kids run from this tent to their playhouse as I try to strafe them. I am drinking real strong coffee which I made ten minutes ago as part of my save-the-afternoon mode, but I haven't typed a single job letter.

The kids dart into their tent and dry themselves by rolling on an old padded U-Haul blanket, and then they jump up and peek back out at me. Calvin is fearless and skips back and forth in the yard, relishing the flashes of chilly water. Janey is playing it safe. She's excited, hopping up and down every time Calvin runs back to dry off, but she has only ventured out once or twice.

I am quite divided. One part directs the hose to douse my youngsters and the other seems to float above the scene and watch. This is what I get. This is the extent of my new life, watering the tender children in my own yard, a golf pro sitting in a green chair, drinking coffee strong enough to chatter his molars, while his wife builds her world around the only Russian in the region to own a chain of pizza parlors. I smile. It's what you do with rue, don't you know: you smile. I smile at Janey's secret face peering through the seams of the tent. I smile at Calvin's bold grin, his body glistening in the sunlight. At two, he is already a good runner. Janey is as self conscious as I am, poor creature, and she has words for things. "Oh my god! Oh my god!" she cries every time Calvin returns. And then she tries a variation from TV: "Thank god you're here!" It's all quite dramatic. She pokes her pretty face out and sees her father again. "Oh my god!" she says, her voice suffused with a nurse's concern, a sister's love.

After a long era of being on hold, a period during which we waited for the next thing to happen in our household, things have begun to shift. Everybody in my family is shaking out. Calvin starts: he has three emergencies a week. He falls off the kitchen counter, having left no evidence of how he achieved the weird height. He is now a tough kid to watch—I mean, he disappears. You'll have him underfoot and turn to pour a cup of coffee: he's gone. You'll find him beneath the bathroom sink checking out the Drano or sitting cross-legged beside the milk in the fridge, the door about to close. Janey has become a smart aleck and says "Sick!" to anything her mother or I say. We were worried about her fitting in and now she's some-how become the leader of the pack at school and is busy not letting other kids fit in. And Tina. My wife has changed wardrobes. She goes to lunch twice a week with friends and talks it over. She may be sorry she married a golfer. She may be through with motherhood. I watch her when I can.

•

My work has run its course, though I don't talk about it. I went in with Mitch, Tina's brother, on a sad nine-hole course at the edge of town, and now it's closed. As Mitch said the day he carted the TV out of the clubhouse: "How much golf can there be? There can only be so much golf." But that wasn't exactly it. The Golf Center at Ten-Acres was trouble from the start. We got a deal on the property, at least Mitch told me it was a deal. He knew I had the last of my prize money in the bank, and I think now he knew what we were getting into. But I should have seen it. I should have been alerted simply by the weird yellow color of the fairways and the cloying stench that rose from every bunker. The course was riddled with bumps, and of course later I was able to witness the garbage emerging: the tires, the home appliances. But for a long while I thought it might be all right. We tried. I'm not a good pro and Mitch is no host, but we tried. I knew we were finished when one day on the fourth green, waiting for three dentists to putt out, the small pond beside the fairway caught fire. The next day I just stayed home and mowed the lawn and edged and raked. That was that. Some days now I water the kids.

Roger Alguire is our eighty-year-old neighbor. He was the first television weatherman in this city. He began weather reporting in 1953 and then was the regular weatherman from 1955 until a few years ago. Roger is a tall, handsome man with resplendent wavy white hair who is no longer recognized in Fry's or Safeway as the weatherman. He is recognized as the tall man who spends his evenings in the local parks with his metal detector, scanning the ground for lost coins. He used to be seen every night with his wife, Gretchen, who was also tall, and who also had a metal detector she swung over the sandy ground. They made an exotic couple in the park, darkness about to fall, moving rhythmically along the paths and through the playground, their postures somehow noble and aloof like rare animals feeding in the twilight. From time to time, Roger would kneel and fork something from the soil and drop it into the large pockets of his trousers.

One night Roger and Gretchen showed us their treasures. After dinner, Tina left our front door open and we went across the street. This was just before Tina started dressing for her lunches. In an empty bedroom, Roger and Gretchen displayed their findings on a wall of bookshelves. The money was in mason jars: bottles of pennies, nickels, dimes, quarters, half a jar of fifty-cent pieces, and stacks of silver dollars. There was a shelf of tools, pliers and screwdrivers, and a shelf of nuts and bolts in peanut butter jars. On one shelf were seven pistols, cleaned and polished, and beside them twenty knives of every sort. On a velvet drape hundreds of gold and silver rings, many with stones. Beside the rings were four feet of pins and brooches. Four directional compasses, a dozen watches, and a shelf of unidentifiable *parts* of things, little springs and levers. On one side were the one-of-a-kind items: an alarm clock, a tall silver trophy with a motorcycle on top, a silver cup inscribed with the name "Brian," a folding shovel, a toy locomotive, and a shiny brass whistle. There was more. Everything had been cleaned and laid out beautifully.

"We've found just over a thousand dollars, U.S. money," Roger said. They had a ledger. "Money isn't very hard to find."

"A thousand dollars," Tina said.

"People don't respect their change anymore," Gretchen said. "They throw it on the street."

"It's not the money," Roger said. "It's the *finding*." He waved his long arm at the shelves of bright objects. "These things would be lost. We found them. That's the excitement."

Gretchen smiled. She was a steady friend to him and shared all this. "And it gets us out of the house every night."

Okay, it was my money and Mitch made the deal. There is a picture of us putting up the sign: Golf Center at Ten-Acres. I liked the idea of owning a course, but I was never a good pro. I'm a good golfer and enjoy the game. At the University of Houston I was number one my last two years, and after that the three years I toured I paid my way plus banking almost ninety thousand. But I can't chat. There are too many times when I don't know what to say. Some guy will chip from sixty yards and bump the flag and I don't have a phrase. Some guy fanning in the trap, one, two, three, and so? What should I say? I've played with those clever guys, quick and funny, but it's not me. There is a lot of pain in nine holes—three guys looking at you, waiting for a word.

When Gretchen died, about a year ago, we lost touch with Roger for a while. He wasn't in the parks and we didn't see him much. Things were different for us then, we were busy with a toddler and getting Janey settled in school and I was still going out to the Golf Center at Ten-Acres. Our golf carts were always getting flats—nails, screws, metal slivers—and I spent a lot of time repairing them. Tina hadn't started having her lunches. We were just a family. I went over to Roger's house a week after the funeral and asked if I could give him a hand with anything, and he shucked me off civilly, just as I would have done to him in the same spot. It was all "How you doing?" and blustery goodwill, and in five minutes I was on the porch shaking hands and backing off.

Then a few weeks later, I started seeing him when I'd take Janey over to the big swings in the park some nights. He wandered alone, head down, listening for the whine of metal and watching the dial on his apparatus: green light for good metal, red for junk. He'd be there when we left. Some nights if I was out in the car I saw him along the canal in the dark, and once taking the sitter home after Tina and I had been to a movie, I saw him working his way across a vacant lot by the railroad tracks. It was midnight.

When you fail, even when it is something easily foreseen and almost expected, even if it is not exactly failure at all, but some sour mix of stupidity, bad luck, and betrayal involving a golf course, even then, if you are a grown man with two little kids who seem headed for harm, and a mortgage that predicts with fiduciary certainty that you will lose your house in six months, when this kind of failure descends upon you, a freshly unemployed golf pro, you will look up from your pillow at your wife as she comes in late another night from some job interview, some rendezvous, with her new employer, Sergei Primalov, a king of franchisers, a pizza czar, and before she drops her skirt to the floor, you will feel the wires cross in your heart and go hot with feelings you don't even know about.

Roger Alguire called me one day, this was six months or so after he'd buried his wife, Gretchen. The kitchen was still his wife's kitchen; it had the feel of a woman. I've been in bachelor's places and they don't have the towels, the ceramics, the sense this is a room in which things have been cooked and cleaned for years and years. A bachelor's kitchen is not about the stove; it is about the fridge.

"Something's going on," he said. "And I need to talk to you." He sat me down and poured the coffee. "There's no surprise in this really," he told me, pushing the ceramic creamer to me. "We were married fifty-two years. Multiply it out, all those days. We knew each other. We . . ." Here Roger stopped and reset himself, lifting both hands from the table. "We could tell what each other was thinking."

I must have been nodding, because he said, "No, I don't think you understand. We could read each other's minds. These last few years we barely needed to speak. There were times . . ." Roger rose and poured us both another drop of coffee. My cup was still full. "There is going to be a message. She's going to be in touch."

Before I could react, he went into the garage and brought back three ancient golf clubs. They were wooden shafts, a wedge, a putter, and an eight iron, the heads deeply rusted. "I found these in the park, on the same path we used to walk. A foot deep. They weren't there before." He handed them to me. "Will you let me look around your golf course?"

It was a nice kitchen, really, a sunny room in the back of the house. There were a lot of ceramics on the windowsill, squirrels and rabbits, and there were two red roosters on the wall. I didn't know what to say to Roger Alguire. The four or five times it has mattered in my life, I have not known what to say. There isn't a quick comeback or the right word in me. I told him I'd help him. I told him of course he could dig around on the Golf Center at Ten-Acres.

The only clue that Tina has given me in the seven years we have been wed is a clue that she has given me about seventy times and the clue is: "I thought things were going to be different than this." Unfortunately, I know what she means. She thought it was going to be great to be married to a golfer. She liked the tour and she liked the clothes you wear in such places and she liked her plans for me. I had been the only quiet man she'd ever dated and I now know she mistook it for something it is not. She didn't know that life was a little too public for me. Many nights, as she dresses to go out I hang around the bedroom waiting for other clues. There will be other clues.

On a windy day, I drive Roger Alguire out to the Golf Center at Ten-Acres. I haven't been out in a while, and more things are missing. Mitch has taken all the carts, of course, and the tools from the repair shed are gone. They weren't his. The clubhouse is still intact—that's my lock. I can still see Mitch in there when we first opened. The foursomes would stagger off the ninth, choking and nauseous from a day of Ten-Acre fumes, and there would be

Mitch in the clubhouse, his hand on the beer tap, grinning like a buffoon. Well, they all hurried by the window to their cars. He didn't sell two kegs of beer the whole year we were in business.

Today the breeze helps and we only catch periodic whiffs of the putrid chemical smell, an aroma like something dead and treated. Both ponds are dry and I see the rear end of what looks like a Studebaker emerging from the center of the small one. There is a lot more junk climbing out of the ground on every fairway and the greens are riddled with new mounds. The Golf Center at Ten-Acres. Roger Alguire ignores all this and simply adjusts the dials on his metal detector and starts off the first tee. The grass is still a vibrant eerie yellow-green, feeding on some rare fuel.

I remember when things started to go bad, I stopped one day at the hardware in Casa Mirage for painting masks we could sell in the clubhouse. I asked the clerk there what he knew about the golf course and he told me it was built on the old Ocotillo landfill. "It was bad," he said. "Golf won't save that property."

Roger calls to me from the middle of the fairway and I hustle down there with a shovel. It seems ridiculous and useful at once. He's got something on the meter, a small shape. Off to one side some huge bald thing is rising through the turf; it looks like the top of a bus. After a minute with the spade, I've uncovered, along with a wicked mess of thin copper wire, a metal tackle box. We kneel on the lawn and Roger opens it.

I don't know if there are any clues about people in the way they dress to go out. Some woman selects clothes from her closet and you're not going. It brings out the child in a person. When she is getting dressed and you're not going, it always seems portentous. Why that skirt, those new pantyhose? You've been wondering about her anyway and it's time to bring it up, the wondering. How will you do it? It's not an easy thing to bring up, really. You've lost your job or it lost you, some emptiness, and you're hanging around the house all day. When the phone rings it is not for you. You're a visitor here who happens to take care of the kids. How will you confront your wife with your feelings? Some night after you've been out digging up your own golf course, bring it up. Try it some time, when your ego is ashrivel, flaccid as an attitude in hell, go in and call the question.

"Tina," I say. She's pulling a powder-blue sweater over her camisole.

"Where's Calvin?" she asks, her head still inside the wool, her naked underarms in my face. She's impatient to be gone, having had the kids all day for the first time in five months.

I go into the kitchen and check the refrigerator first and then spot a movement in the living room. He's squeezed between the couch and the window, pinching flies. I hoist him to my hip and walk back into the bedroom. Tina has shaken out her hair now and is brushing it sharply one way and then the next.

"Tina, are you jogging the back nine?" I say. She brushes her hair, wincing with each stroke.

"Which course would that be?" she says, clapping the brush into the drawer and closing the drawer with her hip. But it is too late. Her hair shines and snaps like a prize animal's, a pony, something at a show where there will be ribbons. She knows which course; she knows the phrase from when we were first married and on the pro tour. On off days men in their ridiculous jogging suits would jog the fairways, their chins erect, unwittingly announcing that they'd taken a woman while on tour. They were new again: look, I can run.

"What's in your heart?" I ask, a stupid question in a blind moment from the cliff's edge, and Calvin squirms on my hip and says, "Dad," as if objecting to something, but Tina doesn't even turn my way. I look at Tina looking at herself in the mirror. My wife. She looks good in blue.

When you fall apart, when you crumble, it doesn't happen all at once, and you don't know about it the way you've known about others who have suddenly cracked up. In fact, for weeks it only feels like too much coffee, too much pizza, not enough sleep, but you wonder if anything is the matter, if there is damage, so you look around for any signs and there are none for you to see, nothing crooked in your landscape. So listen: the way to tell is if you ever say *no problem*. Listen to hear if you say *no problem*.

As I said, things are shifting. Tina is busy. She has a leather daytimer and she's at it all the time, the phone pinched to one shoulder, writing things down. Her calendar thickens. After our little interview, I try to gather enough of myself together to keep from going absolutely down the drain. I watch Calvin as best I can and keep him from harm. It's diverting. He is a kid uninterested in

TV; no ten hours of cartoons for this guy. If I turn it on and stand and watch half of a soft-drink commercial, Calvin is down the block and half over somebody's pool fence. Calvin likes the *back* of the TV, and I have found him back there several times, licking the terminals: audio in, video in. Sometimes, I'll just put him on my shoulders and tour the house imagining our furniture on the driveway in the final garage sale.

At two-thirty, we walk over, Calvin and I, and meet Janey at school. She taught us early not to wait near her door. We are to stand at the corner of the schoolyard and we are not to wave and call her name. This is *major,* she told us. Her class spills out of the door and I see Jane gather her minions around her, six or seven first-grade girls, and they talk in a circle for a moment and then she dismisses them and eventually saunters over to us. Most days Calvin has escaped me by then and he's halfway to her. "Sick," she says as he grabs her arm. "This is really sick. Dad, can't you control your own kids?" Calvin loves this behavior and he grins and falls down and gets up and laughs and laughs. Janey laughs too, but between breaths, she says, "Oh, sick, just sick."

I see a lot of Roger Alguire. He's back to life, commuting with his metal detector to and from the Golf Center at Ten-Acres. He's working through the second green and onto the third hole, and he wears a goofy straw hat festooned with the fishing lures from his first find. Mornings I see him head out as I'm walking Janey to school, and he waves. Some mornings he waits and Calvin and I go with him.

•

I don't care how dumb you are, dumbest among men, so dumb you voluntarily sign over your high-five-figure bank account to your brother-in-law to buy a golf course that smells night and day like a dead thing, even if you are that dumb, when your wife starts seeing another man, although there is no tangible change to point to, no physical trait or blemish, you will know. If she is your woman and you are dumb in a major way, dumb as a stone, a sandpile, a dirtclod, a tongue-tied golf pro, you will still know. And you will know who it is, even if you have never met the man or heard his name, or seen an ad for the chain of pizza parlors he owns. You'll be watering the kids one day in the front yard, and three will go to four o'clock and you will go in for another cup of real strong coffee, and when you return the whole afternoon will tell you: you're not a viable part of the picture anymore, your wife has a new orbit.

There is a strange thing happening at the Golf Center at Ten-Acres. It is a heavy spring day, the clouds piled in ripe gray loads as far as I can see. Roger Alguire drifts slowly across the fourth green, squinting in concentration at his metal detector. Calvin follows him holding on to a piece of rope tied to Roger's belt. There are a few brief powerful gusts before the rain and Roger turns to me where I stand in the sand trap leaning on the shovel and says, "Blow wind!"

"Blow wind!" Calvin says. For a moment they both lift their heads to the sky, listening. The first fat drops sizzle into the sand, and I turn back to where the fourth fairway lies like a minefield of little holes. A newcomer would think we've got real moles. But then he'd see the strange thing. Clear back to the first tee I can see other men wandering the grass, some on their knees prying at the soil, almost a dozen of them searching for things at the Golf Center at Ten-Acres. Four have already come over and asked if I was the owner and paid me five dollars. On the sign Mitch and I erected last year, it is listed as the greens fee.

Calvin squeals in the falling rain and runs toward me across the bumpy green, avoiding a bicycle handlebar protruding from the grass. "I've always loved the rain," Roger says, walking over to me. "But, of course, as a weatherman you can never say that."

Tina has taken a job. She is the new manager, not assistant manager nor manager-in-training, but *manager* of Sergei's Pizza. I thought she was going to be a legal secretary. When she'd go to lunch, she always dressed like a legal secretary. I thought business school. I thought tutoring. No. She runs Sergei's, twelve hours a day, six days a week. And as she frankly put it to me the second night of her job, the second night she came in at one-thirty: it means we may get to keep the house.

All the other things, the things I would like to say, to know, I can't ask: does Sergei come by? Has he ever touched you? These questions lack something. They shrivel in the shadow of the question of our house. A house is a big thing which guards your furniture from the weather and provides some quiet from the world.

•

When I was a kid, seven, eight, nine years old, I used to watch Roger Alguire do the weather on Channel Four. It all came back to me when we first moved in here and I found out who he was. In those days his hair was white only on the sides and he wore classy tweed jackets and a tie and he really moved around the weathermap. He had markers and drew the fronts with arrows, and the pressure areas with circles. He also drew lightning and spirals and little triangles for precipitation. He wasn't like a pal or a coach or some kind of lost host for the climate, the way the guys are today. He had an earnest grace that made him seem complicit in the creation of the weather. You believed him. When he drew the arrow, it made you get ready.

When Tina comes home, she smells faintly of Parmesan cheese, a pale, rank odor, the smell of after-sex. Parmesan cheese is okay by itself, but you don't want to smell it on your wife. She rustles out of her clothing and slips into bed heavily. We haven't touched for weeks. The sour smell of cheese makes me nothing more than weary.

There is a lot of pizza around our house. Russian pizza, two slices in a baggie, half a pie in the white cardboard box, a grinning Lenin on the cover. Tina uses our house for only two things now—to leave excess pizza and to store her wardrobe. I told Tina good for her, that I was glad we would keep the house, that she was alive again after six years with me, but that I didn't want the kids going to Sergei's. I don't want them to run around in a big pizza place and ride the little rides or beg for tokens for the games, and I don't want them ever in this lifetime to meet Sergei Primalov.

Mornings, after Janey has gone to school, Calvin and I take cold pizza over to Roger Alguire's while Tina sleeps. We have breakfast with him. The Russian makes a whole wheat crust for his pizza and it is wonderful cold with a glass of milk. Roger thrives; he's got the Golf Center at Ten-Acres mapped out and he's halfway through the sixth hole, a dogleg that runs by one of the dry ponds. He eats his pizza with gusto and washes it down with hot tea. He doesn't ask me about Tina—hasn't for weeks now—so that tells me he's as sharp as ever. He and Calvin are buddies in these morning pizza feasts, and they sit together in one chair. Calvin's picked up one of Janey's phrases, "Are we having fun, or what?" and when he says this, Roger laughs and laughs. At eight-thirty, we go out to the Golf Center at Ten-Acres.

When your wife doesn't come home one night, and you call her at work the next day and she says she's real busy and, incidentally, she's real happy, but she can't talk right now, and no, she says, she won't be home tonight either, you will have an odd thought, perhaps your first thought: Well, who didn't know that, you'll think. That's no surprise to me.

Like any other person in that spot, eleven in the morning, I put the receiver back on the wall phone in the kitchen and I look at it for what, a couple minutes. It's your right to look at your phone for as long as you want. Finally, I say something aloud. I say, "No problem."

•

Calvin and I don't join Roger at the Golf Center at Ten-Acres. What I do is go into Roger's house and take the rusty .38 caliber pistol from the shelf. He's oiled it and it will function. Calvin and I drive to Redtent Discount and buy a box of shells. On the way to Mitch's, every block, the weight of what I am doing increases. Until this drive, I have been well measured. I haven't sighed hard or said son of a bitch, but I cannot put any of what is happening back together again and I'm losing my way. I imagine the scene: I will stop at Mitch's condo, walk by the pool, go up the stairs, ring his buzzer, and when he answers I will put the old pistol under his chin and shoot him fully through the head.

We pull into the lot. It's jammed with Saabs and BMWs. I've got the .38 under my seat. The parking lot is full on a weekday. These people don't work. Suddenly something smells as if we were at the Golf Center at Ten-Acres. Calvin has got the cigarette lighter and is printing burning circles in the seat.

But the sick truth in the sick pit of my stomach is that I don't really want to see Mitch. Ever. And, regardless of your anger, regardless of your rage, regardless of some other thing like electricity gone wrong in your golfer's brain, you cannot drive over and shoot your relatives. For one thing, there's Calvin. You can't drive your children over to shoot people. You're going to need a sitter.

Golf is a game full of tactical decisions, most of them so small and automatic that you hardly realize you're making them. At every distance and at every incline and turning, you decide whether to cut it close or go around, which club to use, how hard to swing. But the truth is there is no real tough stuff. You never have to decide, for example, somewhere on the seventh fairway to turn around and play back through six. It is a game with a clear etiquette and the rules are followed. Things are kept quiet and the person furthest from the hole plays first. The greens are smooth as felt and the traps are raked to look as if you were the first one to make a mistake. It is not a game to prepare young people for the simmering rigors of marriage and mortgage. It has not prepared me.

After one full night of thought, a night wandering our house, room by room, checking on the kids, sitting on the bed and then every chair in turn, and then the lawn furniture as the dawn came up, an old .38 pistol in my lap, trying to think of the one thing I could do to make things even a tiny bit better, I make a tough decision.

I put all of Tina's clothing in the street. It is a quiet activity which I do with thoroughness. By sunrise I have done a careful job, folding the clothing neatly into stacks at the edge of the street. Tina has a lot of clothes. Roger Alguire comes out to get his paper and he calls to me. "Looks like no more pizza."

"We've had our share," I say. I want to go inside before the huge pile of clothing can make me sad.

"When the kids get up, come over for some eggs," he says. "And bring back my pistol," he adds. "Before you hurt yourself."

The parking lot at the Golf Center at Ten-Acres is full when we arrive at nine. I've never seen it full in my life. Men and women are scattered all over the nine holes, scanning the course and digging here and there. A group of five sit on the lip of the trap along the second green and watch a man trying to wrestle something from the ground. Behind them two hundred yards I can see a man and a woman circling in the rough beside the ninth fairway, their metal detectors poised. They have found something. The pocked greens and fairways today emit a different odor, less sour, something. It actually smells like Tina when she gets a permanent, toasty and serious. Several people wave at Roger and three guys come up to me opening their wallets.

By noon the clubhouse is full. I'm frying burgers and Roger is serving drinks, pop and beer. I still have a beer license. I've spent the morning filling a cigar box with greens fees and keeping an eye on Calvin. Janey walks up and back in front of the clubhouse like a hostess. On or near all the little tables are the *things* my patrons are finding in the ground. Carburetors, desk lamps, silverware. It is Saturday. Through the windows I can see hundreds of people wandering the Golf Center at Ten-Acres.

Sometime in the midafternoon there is a scream. I've let my guard down and begun smiling, and when I hear the scream I know in a second it's Janey and that everything is up in the air again. "Dad! Dad! Dad!" Janey screams, running into the room and collapsing on my knees. "Oh thank god!" Several people look over. "Dad. I've got to tell you something," Janey goes on, her face now practical, the nurse.

"Good," I say. "Here I am."

"Dad," she says, putting her hand on my wrist like a counselor, "Calvin ate some pennies." She points out where Calvin stands on the practice green, his chin down.

Outside I lift him up and ask, "Did you put some pennies in your mouth?"

He clips his chin tighter against his chest.

It's a bad moment. I hear the tinkling of fishing lures on a hat, and Roger Alguire is at my side. He takes Calvin from me. "Did my boy eat some money?" he says and Calvin hugs him around the neck. As he does, his fists unclench and a few pennies spill to the green.

Calvin will do anything Roger says, so that when he's instructed to lie on the grass, he gets right on his back, his arms straight along his sides. Roger sits on the bench and holds the metal detector across his lap. He is adjusting the controls. "I didn't mean this to happen to your golf course," he says, nodding out at all the people. "I just need more time. I'm eighty and I need more time to adjust to everything. We were married forever. This is all new to me." He stands up. "Are you ready, Calvin, my boy?"

Calvin's eyes go large and he nods.

I love my son, but I start to float again, to rise above the scene as Roger steps on one of the fallen pennies and places the head of the device over his foot. The metal detector whines. "Okay," he says. "Are we having fun, or what?" Several people have come up to the edge of the practice green to watch the demonstration. I look down on all of this, my children, my new life. What I wanted is not possible. Now, here above my riddled desert property I see that I wanted fifty-two years, someone to finish sentences for me.

"It's all right, Calvin," Janey says. "It's an experiment." Calvin lies still and beautiful on the lumpy practice green. My neighbor Roger Alguire runs the head of his metal detector slowly over the little boy from head to toe and back again. Things have stopped for a moment as people look up from their digging here at the Golf Center at Ten-Acres.

THE SUMMER OF
VINTAGE CLOTHING

Ruth was dressing for Vicky's party when Carl came home and told her he had lost the turkey. She lowered both ends of her necklace and looked at him. She thought: Of course you did. It was a big moment there in the bedroom, Ruth sitting on the bed, Carl standing before her, frowning in concentration, his palms out, and before he could shift his weight or begin anything, she saw him as if for the first time, her husband, a handsome man who had been bright and clever and who was still a good lawyer, but who was, as he stood pantomiming what he might have done with the smoked turkey for Vicky's party, a man who had spent years growing vague.

Carl thought hard. "I'm in Canyon Market off of Foothill . . ."

"Can you help me with this?" Ruth handed him the necklace. It was a string of small copper disks which they had purchased on last year's trip to the Yucatán. Carl looked at it now as if it were a puzzle, and Ruth could see his mind was somewhere else.

Carl had been her mainstay; at one time she had counted on him. But now he was gone, lost in another battle with

Gerver, totally preoccupied with his own stress. He came home these days and *did TV*—smoking his cigars, shoes on the couch—that being his phrase as he raised a hand to quiet whatever question she might ask: "Not now, honey, okay? I'm doing TV here, do you see?" On the screen a man would be pressing both fists into his eyes trying to think on *The Family Feud, things at a wedding shower*. And after doing TV, Carl came to bed and wanted to mount her like a moment's information, a newsbreak. There had been times like this before in this marriage, and as soon as Carl or Gerver relented, changed their memos, shook hands, he would be back for a while and she could rely on him again. Now Ruth sat on the bed and looked at Carl as he tried to figure out why he had a necklace in his hands.

But it was her son Sean, a boy best described by the ridiculous phrase "the apple of her eye," who had Ruth most upset. It was what she had heard him say. He'd always been interesting and funny and companionable, a friend in the house really, willing to talk at night sometimes if there was popcorn or ice cream and Carl was asleep on the couch. They'd watch TV together and comment on the characters, and Sean was always surprising her with his observations. "You can tell the total mental state of a person by watching him in the left-turn lane," and during love scenes he'd point at the screen and say, "It's some kind of bonding maneuver, as far as I can tell." Some-times he would remove his sleeping father's shoes and say, "Dad, you've got to learn to respect the furniture." And sometimes it was Ruth who slept on the couch, or feigned sleep, lying deeply in the cushions to hear Sean tell Carl about the track coach or the debate trip. Those nights covered her like a blanket and she could feel the soft electricity of it in the backs of her legs, too much and not enough at the same time, these men, talking.

This was the summer of vintage clothing. Sean and his friend David were into old clothes. They'd raid the Deseret Industries thrift shops and come home in three-piece suits and wide silk ties handpainted with animals and birds. Sean mowed the lawn in vests and the two boys played tennis in pleated trousers. It was Ruth's joy to see the two of them on lounge chairs in the backyard like two barefoot bankers, their ties loosened in the sun. Eventually they'd carefully disrobe, hanging their garments on the pool furniture until the baggy trousers came off revealing their swimsuits, and they'd dive into the blue water.

Lately there had been a third in this game, Dorie, also a sophomore at Suburban, a girl Ruth liked, though it was unclear whose friend she was. David was smoother, more confident and gregarious, but Sean was tall and—the only word Ruth could think of—pretty in a Ricky Nelson kind of way. Dorie was over two or three times a week in flowered skirts and billowy blouses looking like something prime for a country weekend, sometimes a blue or beige suit, the jacket and tight skirt making her look ready to go off to the office. "This hat," Dorie would say. "Fifty cents." And she'd turn to show the large straw hat, its band a colorful wrap of red silk.

Mostly Ruth wasn't included. She watched the three young people from her kitchen window. They tuned the radio to KOY, a station that played only music from the forties and fifties, Patti Page, Robert Goulet, Glenn Miller, Tony Bennett; it was hilarious. Ruth's friend Vicky stood with her one day at the sink watching the young people and said, "I love coming over here. It makes me feel so *young.*" That day at the window, Vicky had said, "They think they're in a movie. I remember it, the feeling. You sit around with your fingers under your chin waiting for someone to ask you what's the matter. It's the age of love-liness. Everything is terribly important and terribly lovely."

The women watched Dorie stand and slowly unbutton the front of her blouse and place it on the back of her chair. She moved to the pool's edge and stood for a dive. Vicky said, "Who is that?" Dorie swam in a sleek one-piece that showed her more woman than Ruth would have imagined.

Your son is fifteen, Ruth thought. He is fifteen this summer and you are the iced-tea lady now. In three years he'll be gone. And she was the iced-tea lady, kidding them about their getups as she set the large plastic tumblers on the small tables by the pool. They can't even see me, she thought, I'm just the source of iced tea. Sometimes she hummed along with the ridiculous music. She watched them from her window with nothing as much as pure feeling, three beautiful kids in the sunshine, dressed for the forties.

It was vintage everything, really. The word itself came out almost too often. David would appear at their door in a brown suit two sizes too large and wave a videocas-sette, saying, "This is a classic. This is vintage Karloff." The young people watched old films in the den, black-and-white horror films, and lounged so deeply in the fur-niture it was as if they were hiding. When Ruth came through the room from time to time, she looked for clues about who was with whom, but the alliances were never clear. Some days Dorie lay out on the couch like an actress, the boys in the two big chairs, some days she sat with David there, and then some days she sat on the floor in front of Sean's chair. Ruth would watch for a moment, the Mummy stepping heavily through the open terrace doors or Dracula opening his caped arms and turning into a bat. She liked having the kids around the house, though they couldn't see her, but she could tell things were changing. The nights Sean would go down to David's for dinner or a movie, she would work at her desk, pretend to, and then double-check the porch light. It was hard to read. She wasn't used to this new thing, waiting for her son to return.

And then, of course, something snapped. Last night as Ruth was rinsing her serving tray, she heard through her open window her son talking to David in the blue night of the backyard. Over the humming of the pool filter pump, Sean was speaking, his voice printed on her life forever, and she heard the words before she had a chance to disbelieve them: "Yeah," she heard him say. "She is such a cunt." Ruth felt her elbows take fire and weaken, and she put down the tray in her hands.

"Okay, okay," Carl went on. "I can get this." But he wasn't talking about the necklace. "I spoke to the butcher and he said that it would be a minute, then I ran into Vicky." Carl had forgotten about the necklace in his hand and was gesturing, setting up imaginary places in the grocery store. He was being logical and retracing his steps. "And she said something about something . . ."

"She said she'd see us tonight at the party and that we're going to meet her new boyfriend, the Texan." Ruth took the necklace back from him and tried to fasten it again.

"Right. That's it." Then Carl looked at her with surprise. "And she said Tom Gerver's coming. His wife is one of your accounts? Something."

"That's right."

Carl shook off the distance and said, "Okay, so the butcher handed me the bag over the counter." Carl hoisted the imaginary bag. "And when I went up front to check out I found I didn't have any cash. . . ." Here Carl thrust his hands into his pockets until he fished out a paper slip. "So I put it on Visa." He paused and read the slip very slowly: "Smoked turkey: thirty-four forty-four."

"What's the program?" Sean said, dropping a shoulder against their doorway. He was wearing a brown suit vest over a white T-shirt. His trousers were cinched tight around his narrow waist, but they still sagged. "Who's feeding you guys tonight?"

Ruth had avoided him since last night, and now with the sound of his voice she felt her heart contract. "We'll be at Vicky's," she said carefully. "What are your plans?"

Sean took two steps to Ruth and lifted the necklace from her hands. Deftly he dipped it around her neck and had it fastened before she could move.

Carl was still in the grocery store. "There was a girl behind me with a new baby, and," Carl turned to where she would have stood, "I helped her."

"I'll be here," Sean said. "David and Dorie may come over."

"And I took the baby." Now Carl's hands were really full. "It was raining . . . her car was next to mine." Carl seemed to be reading off the ceiling. "She opened the door—it's a two-door—and I put the baby in his car seat in the back."

"Dad, you are such a hero."

"And . . . I . . ." Carl dropped his arms and sat on the bed. "God, I don't know. I drove home. I don't know where it is. I lost the turkey."

"Want me to check the car?"

"No, I've been through it six times."

"It doesn't matter," Ruth said, feeling her neck stiffen. "Call the market and ask them to set aside another. We'll pick it up on the way. Get dressed, Carl. Let's go meet Vicky's friend."

When she stood, Sean said, "You look good, Mom. A little modern, but good. David thinks you're a babe." Ruth left the room. She could hear the men talking behind her.

The theme of the party, Ruth had forgotten, was tequila. There were trays of Shooters and Sunrises and every plate on the buffet had a little card attached that read Tequila something or other, "Tequila Fettucine," "Tequila Jamboree." It was still raining lightly and Vicky's house was crowded with dozens of people. Vicky brought a man over and introduced Ruth and Carl. His name was actually Bo and he was from Houston or near there and he did something with land. Ruth noted Bo's thin mustache, something you rarely saw anymore, something a man does on purpose. A black line along the top of his lip.

As Ruth and Carl laid out their tray, Vicky stuck a little sign, "Tequila Turkey," on the platter. She handed Ruth a sweet Sunrise, which puckered Ruth's mouth. "Battery acid," Vicky said, pointing to the hinge of her jaw. "They give you a little sizzle right there, don't they? Battery acid. You get it from chocolate and beer too." Vicky looked at Ruth and asked, "What's the matter?"

"Nothing. Something. Somebody in our house is fifteen."

"Who? Carl?"

"Funny. We're *doing* growth at our house," Carl said. "You can feel the limits groaning."

Ruth looked at her husband and thought, How would you know?

Tom Gerver came up behind Carl and nodded at Ruth as a greeting. He took Carl by the arm, leading him into the other room, which Ruth could only interpret as a good sign.

"Is Sean still dressing for dinner?" Vicky asked.

Ruth nodded, aware she didn't want to talk about it really. There was something too personal about it, this summer. A moment later Vicky pointed to where Bo was making drinks at the bar table. "So, how do you like him?"

"He seems quite . . . manly."

Vicky smiled. "Don't you hate it," she said. "If it weren't for that trait, they'd be all right. Actually he's a nice guy. A little too willing to please. *Very* considerate. Very . . . in bed it's this and that for three hours. Newly divorced men are like that."

Vicky went over and escorted him into the party. Throughout the evening as Ruth drifted through the rooms, a lot of her friends commented on how tall Sean was now, and there were some funny things said about his costumes, divided between those who thought he had decided to run for office and those who thought he was going into the ministry. Everyone said the word *fifteen* wistfully. "Fifteen," one older woman said. "Wonderful fifteen. It's the first time you'd like to sell them."

Ruth relished being alone at the party, not engaging in long discussions, just wandering from room to room. Several people complimented her on her necklace and she had a feeling she hadn't had in a long time—since parties at her sorority house—that something was going to happen next.

The rain let up sometime after eleven and as groups of people began to venture out onto the back deck, Ruth searched the house for Carl. The doors and windows were open and the fresh cool air seemed like fall. She found him flat on his back in the wet side yard, side by side with his buddy Tom Gerver, both of them absolutely drunk. From the position of their bodies, flung out and imbedded in the grass, it looked as if they had fallen from an airplane.

"Hi honey," Carl said. "Tom and I were taking a break."

As she helped Carl up, Tom said, "You're a good woman, Ruth. He rose to an elbow and said with drunken sincerity, "I'm sorry about your turkey."

Ruth didn't care that Carl was so far gone or that she'd have to drive home. She'd driven him home before and she was relieved that he seemed to have made peace with Tom. When they were in the car, he was chatty. "What's bugging you about Sean?" he asked. "I like his girl-friend." He folded his arms, then finding they didn't fit, refolded them. They were waiting to turn left onto their street.

"How does he know about necklaces?"

"What?" Carl looked at her.

"There's something to know about necklaces," she said.

"What is it? What is there?" Carl pointed down the empty roadway, "You can turn now, Ruth. There's nobody coming."

Ruth measured the turn with exaggerated care. "She's not his girlfriend," she said.

•

At home the house was empty though the television was on. Ruth stood and watched it for a moment—a high-rise building was burning. Carl slumped through the room, his eyes half shut, waving both palms at her and going straight to bed. Ruth sat down and slipped off her shoes. On television now, two blond men smeared with camouflage grease in sleeveless T-shirts, carrying automatic weapons, detonators, and a strange sphere, entered an elevator. This is where Sean would say to her, "Those are the bad guys, Mom." It was one of their jokes—the way she had always talked to him as a child when he watched television. Ruth watched the screen. She had distinctly heard him say it, "She's such a cunt." Several of the upper stories of the building exploded, spraying fans of white sparks into the night.

Leaving the television on, Ruth went into the kitchen and made herself a scotch and water. She wandered back through the house, every room, straightening things in the dark, her desk—so clean already—Sean's bed—neat too—in a room so clearly still a boy's, the walls all athletes and animals, his first debate trophy on the shelf (Carl's phrase, "Your *first*"). In the glowing dark she touched the dish of change on his bureau and then suddenly became self-conscious, her face warm, as if she'd been going through his pockets, and she moved into the hallway and then to the front of the house, making sure again that the porch light was on.

Back in the dark kitchen, she poured another short splash of scotch and went through the French doors onto the pool deck. It was fresh outdoors after the recent rain and she could smell the wet cement as it dried in the night and she could hear the clacking of the palm fronds above the neighbor's yard. She walked out around the pool and sat on the side of the diving board. From here her dark yard and house seemed vast, another landscape. Shapes slowly emerged, the lumps of towels, the deck tables, Sean's suit jacket on the back of a chair.

When she heard the laugh, she felt it as something sharp in her chest and then she heard it again, an alto note that could not be suppressed, and the warmth spread down her arms. "Sean?" she said, her voice strange, ready, and then louder: "Sean?" Now she couldn't hear anything in the mix of the pool pump, the palm fronds' dry whispers. "Sean?" She couldn't see anything in the dark reflections of the water or the windows of the house and she realized she couldn't move either, she couldn't get up right now or walk to the house, it was the strangest feeling and it wouldn't let her speak again either. And for a moment in the liquid night she was that still, not calm, but not panicked either, just kept there by the weight of the two sounds she'd heard and known about all along.

Beneath her she saw the water ripple and heard it lapping at the tile in a new way, then the surface broke in a dark oval which became a face, silver under hair as black and varnished as a movie star's from the twenties. She didn't recognize him at first, his face, until he reached for the side of the pool and she saw his wrist and forearm.

"Sean?"

"Yeah. Mom, hi. Party over?" His voice was thick, husky, a whisper.

"Is that David?" Ruth looked out into the dark where she knew Dorie hid in the water.

"No, he just left," Sean said. He was treading water, staying away from her.

"It's after midnight, Sean."

"Really. Okay."

Ruth now heard Dorie's body rise from the water, the short rush of water in the far dark, and before her son's next plaintive "Mom?"—a word so saturated with pleading that she found it almost repulsive—the light in the kitchen went on around the shape of her husband. The light fell in a cartoonish square across the patio and Ruth saw Dorie stand casually as if to meet it, so casually it hurt, and drop the towel the way she would if alone after a shower, her body here only white, her arms, her high breasts white, as she lifted her shift over her head and began to wriggle into it.

"Mom?" her son said again from the water.

But coming out of the house like a figure in a horror film now, in an old pair of pajama bottoms and carrying a liter bottle of Perrier, was her husband, and he said, "Ruth? Ruth? I put it in her car." He became a dark shadow before her. He didn't know his son drifted in the water at his feet nor was he aware of the girl dressing behind him—who now knelt and busily worked at her shoes.

Ruth said nothing and then she said, "Carl."

"It's raining in the parking lot. Do you see, I know what happened." He gestured with the bottle of water and his free hand.

"When the girl flopped the front seat forward so I could reach in and put the baby in the car seat—see it? It's raining. The ground is wet. I put the bag on the floor there behind the front seat."

There was movement behind Carl and Ruth saw Dorie slip out the side gate. She could see beneath her in the water, like some creature, Sean, his white eyes, in a scene that was now only black-and-white. She stood up.

"Hey," Carl said. "Is that Sean?"

And Ruth felt then the whole world take hold and her heart, her body flood with wonder. And even though she tried, she couldn't stop from taking half a step back like an actress in a bad film, her hands raised in defense, in denial, as her eyes actually widened. She saw it; she saw it all. She saw these strangers. It was stark and clear. And she had been brought here from some other place at this point in her life, forty years of age, to live with them.

PLAN B
FOR THE
MIDDLE CLASS

Everybody's three. Harry has just turned three and Ricky won't be four until August, and all I want to do is get Katie in bed. The theme for the spring is sand. It is everywhere. The boys carry it around in their pockets until it pulls their pants down. We don't even notice the sandy trails through the house anymore, and when the two three-year-olds come in for lunch, they squirm in their seats until each lifts a scoop of sand onto the table beside his grilled cheese sandwich. They will not eat until there is sand on the table.

Right now they are both well into their sandwiches and I watch Katie pour milk and move about the kitchen. I can hear the uneven flicker of sand filtering onto the floor and the sound is magnified by my throat-dry lust. I am trying to restrain myself from going up behind Katie and fondling her breasts. I can sense she's got an eye on me anyway. This sweet hollow call of desire has been growing for months, it seems, years, perhaps it too is three. It's rich. It's as crazy as a song. Just the touch of her sleeve can set me off. Katie brushes the hair off her forehead and looks at me again: "What?" she says.

I turn back into the living room and ask the guy who is fixing the VCR how it's going. He's a house-call guy out of the Nickel Ads. He's young and bald and wearing white overalls. The VCR is out of its shell in four big components on the floor.

"There's a lot of sand in here, buddy," he tells me.

"I know," I say, and he looks up at me for an explanation. "It's been sandy."

"Well," he says, measuring it out like medicine and going back to the pieces of the VCR, "that's hard on the heads. You're going to wear your heads out with sand."

I nod as if to say I understand, I stand corrected, I hear and receive his scolding gratefully, I couldn't agree more. We'll do better.

The truth is that if my parents weren't flying in to be with the kids, I would have poured another cup of sand into the mechanism myself. It has served up a limited repertoire in the two years we've had it. The only movies we see are *Dumbo, Land of the Lost, More Dinosaurs,* and *Using Your Cuisinart.* After two hundred viewings I became numb to *Dumbo,* which is an ardent feminist film. Dumbo has no father, the circus workmen drink away their pay, the Ringmaster is a blustering fool, and the only good man is a mouse. *Land of the Lost* is the hokiest video in the country, drawn from an old television series about a family who take the wrong turn on a raft trip and end up in another world, a world full of dinosaurs, cavemen, the whole show. *More Dinosaurs* and *Using Your Cuisinart* are documentaries.

After dinner every night while I run bathwater, Katie cleans up in the kitchen, and Harry and Rick sop up one of these cinema classics. Harry sits there naked—as he is naked at the lunch table right now—and watches the television through his binoculars. Harry is a naked child all of the time. You can tie his shoes one minute and the next find them along with his shirt et cetera on the front step. But he is never without his binoculars. He holds the big end to his eyes, so things must appear way out there. Other people have told us about their children who resented and avoided clothing, so the fact that Harry is always naked doesn't bother us too much yet. However, his drifting through the house with those glasses held to his face can be disconcerting.

Ricky, on the other hand, isn't interested in his binoculars. He has become, like so many American preschoolers, an absolute paleontologist. He knows all the dinosaurs and all of their cousins. Katie has kept up with all of this, which is no small task, since they've changed all the names and half the theories since we were in school. Except the triceratops; there is still a triceratops.

From time to time, I'll stop on the way home from work and rent a movie, *Body Heat,* or *An Officer and a Gentleman,* figuring we'll watch something with a little sex in it after the boys are in bed and then I'll reach for Katie and we've had a wonderful life that way—one thing leads sweetly to another. But we never see the films. By the time the kids are down, we're shot. The videos stay in their cases on top of the console. Once we tried to watch *Siesta* in the morning while the kids were in the sandbox. Well, that's no good. That's not right. You can't watch movies in the morning.

And now my parents are coming, so they can watch *Land of the Lost.* They haven't seen it yet. They haven't heard Marshall's line as the characters look around at their jungle home: "I think we're in another world."

Back in the kitchen, Harry smiles at me and puts the

large end of his binoculars to his face. He is looking at a full glass of milk that appears to be fifty yards away.

"Boys," I start, "while we're gone and Grandma and Grandpa are here, do not put sand in the television."

Ricky can't hear me. He is full face into his sandwich, all business, his hands working more and more of it into his mouth. Little naked Harry turns and looks at me with his binoculars. "Dad, Dad," he says. I wait for him to finish. I must look like I'm up here ten stories.

And, in fact, I feel remote, my little family way below, another life, another world. I've lost my job. It crumbled under me and now I'm off balance. Perhaps I'm falling, waiting as in a dream to hit the ground, waiting certainly to tell Katie.

"Dad, I got a big one," Harry says, gesturing to the milk and knocking the glass completely over in a quick splash. Katie is there in a second with a sponge almost as if she could sense it coming, the way a good infielder moves to the ball when he sees the bat swing, and the mess which I thought would be major, milk and sand, is nothing in a moment. Rick hasn't stopped eating. When Katie bends down for the last pickup, I can't stop myself, I run my hand across her arched back, and it is then I feel the first pang of something else, an itch, my rash. My jock rash is coming back. I adjust my shorts and scratch myself.

"That's lovely," Katie says, watching me. She sits down with the boys. "No sand," she says, giving each a look in the eye. "No sand in the television."

When I was seventeen, I played varsity baseball for Union High School and I developed my first case of this rash, the case for the record books. There could have been many causes. Just being seventeen is what it was. And wet jocks. You take kids seventeen and make them wear wet jockstraps to play baseball, they'll get something. Jock rash seems the most harmless consequence. The school supplied socks, jocks, and T-shirts, and several times that spring the clothes dryer by the locker room was busted, and we'd take the field against Claremont or Mountain in damp straps. At first I noticed a slight burning and then the visible rash, and then being seventeen and busy, I neglected it the whole term, until I couldn't ignore it anymore. My friend Ryan McBride had the locker next to mine in the team locker room, and one night after a game I lifted the leg of my boxer shorts—we all wore boxer shorts that year—and asked him, "You got any of this?"

"Holy shit, Lew," he said. "You've got a royal case of jock itch. Come here, Baker, look at Lew's crotch!"

At the time, I didn't know that he meant I had it for life. In fact, at the time it didn't sound too bad. It sounded like a kind of compliment: Hey, Lewis, you're a man. Something like that.

It was something to see: a raised red rash running out on each leg in an area about the size of a hand, so tender that the hem of my boxer shorts felt like wire. Nights I would douse it with medicated powder and wake up with my heart beating in the raw flesh. There was no help. Finally my mother asked me what—in heaven—was the matter. I was so desperate I showed her. She wrinkled her nose and called Dr. Wilson, making an appointment for after graduation that I would never have to keep.

•

The video guy is done. He used a little hand-held vacuum cleaner for a while at the end and then snapped the facing back on the VCR and shut his tools. He hands me the ticket: ninety-six dollars. It's worth it. I'm not going to squawk now. In twenty-four hours Katie and I will be in bed in our room at the Royal Hawaiian while in Arizona my parents watch *More Dinosaurs*. Ninety-six dollars is cheap.

"See, boys," I say, "Mr. Waldren"—I read his name from the receipt as I write the check—"has fixed our television. The boys don't want to put sand in the machine, do they, Mr. Waldren."

Mr. Waldren takes the check and folds it into his overalls pocket. He looks up at me and simply says, "Why would they want to do that?"

When I was nine years old, I started reading the newspaper, the comics, the puzzles, and "Ask Andy." My mother would fold the paper to the right page and hand it to me. She encouraged literacy in her household, this farmgirl valedictorian from a Nebraska high school. She always completed the crossword, except for a few easy four- and five-letter words, which I was expected to do, and I remember learning forever the name of the Elbe River in Germany, which appeared with disturbing frequency in the *Salt Lake City Tribune*. But it was "Ask Andy" which really challenged me. "What Do Pandas Eat?" would be the headline, and then in small print after the two-column answer (bamboo shoots, ten pounds a day) would be some kid's name and the fact that she had won a set of encyclopedias for asking about pandas. It seemed obvious that I could do better than the panda question, and I began sending questions to Andy.

My first, I remember, was based on the fact that pandas are related to raccoons. "What Do Raccoons Eat?" I followed that with three other questions about raccoons. "Where Do Raccoons Live?" "Why Do Raccoons Have Masks?" "How Did the Raccoon Get Its Name?" I became, in fact, the fourth-grade expert on raccoons, which my teacher Mrs. Talbot thought was just fine, but Andy did not acknowledge my questions. From North American mammals, I went on to magnetism and sent in a series of bewildering questions about the very essence of matter and its fundamental behavior. Andy was unimpressed. It is not a good thing for an elementary school pupil to send off questions in the mail and get nothing in return, and my mother tried to ease the sting by praising my queries (she typed them) and defending Andy in his difficult work. "He gets lots of letters, honey." Nevertheless, I let Andy go. I stopped reading his column. I just filled in the crossword puzzles with my mother's help and took up clipping "Gasoline Alley."

That summer was Little League and YMCA Camp, and it was at camp months later that I struck on the idea that had been waiting for me. I saw it, I felt it just like Moon Mullins with a light bulb over his head. I mean, I felt the physical shock of having a radical thought. Actually, it happened on our cabin's overnight up the Soapstone Creek. Our counselor, Michael Overholt, a college student and botanical genius, was off collecting and pressing ferns for his collection, and the other campers and myself were having a contest. We were gathered around one huge Douglas Fir (flat needles,) seeing who could pee furthest up the trunk. It was there, leaning backward marking the tree, that I saw the concept that sent me back to "Ask Andy" for the last time.

The rest of camp went by in a blur as I waited to get home and write my letter. I remember falling off a horse on our trail ride, making a black-and-yellow key chain with boondoggle in crafts, and spending most of capture-the-flag in jail. It was all irrelevant to me. I had seen the future.

As was her custom, my mother typed my letter for me. I had to print it first, as always, and though I could tell she didn't think it was a brilliant question, she didn't say anything, just moved to the typewriter (a bad sign) and had me look up the word "urinate," which wasn't much of a task once she let me know it began with a *u*. "Dear Ask Andy, When I urinate, why does it stay in a stream instead of spraying all over the place?" It was my longest letter to Andy, more than twice as long as anything about raccoons, and my mother did say, as she typed the envelope, that its length might hurt it.

I didn't care. It was a great question. And during the next year, fifth grade, I read "Ask Andy" every day. It was a big year for the planets, space in general, with secondary themes of reptiles and mineralogy. There was almost no anatomy or hydrology. It didn't really hurt my feelings. I remember thinking as the spring came that year and baseball started up again: It's okay. No wonder he didn't print my question. *He doesn't know.*

My mother bought a set of *The Book of Knowledge* that year and would buy a set of *Britannicas* the next. There wasn't anything in either about my question, and after a while I got into the mysteries of art, studying all the jungles of Rousseau, the stark dramas of Goya, and then settling on the romantic Delacroix. I would stare at "Liberty

Guiding the People" for hours at a time in *The Book of Knowledge*. Her blouse is torn down, as you know, but it isn't a moment for niceties. If she stopped to cover herself, the battle could be lost. I was in the sixth grade by then and I found the painting compelling. I couldn't get her courage and nudity into my head at the same time, and burned with curiosity about such things. But it came to me from time to time as I'd write ELBE in the crossword puzzles, which my mother was leaving more and more blank for me to do: I'd stumped Andy. I had this picture of some guy who looked like Mr. Drubay, my arithmetic teacher, standing in his little office which was stacked high with envelopes of questions as he looked out the window at a big city and scratched his head. He wasn't happy. There were probably a lot of things he didn't know, things he would never know. I feel that way more and more myself. He probably worried about being fair giving out the encyclopedias. So I ended that year thinking about that confused guy in his office and staring at Liberty's beautiful breasts amid all the damage and the danger. I'd stumped Andy. All I could think was: If there were an answer for every question, what kind of world would it be?

I am told that one of my strengths as "Zoo Lewis," in my column "Animals Unlimited," is the patience I display toward obvious questions. In my eleven years I've received four Press Service Awards for the column, "for making the obvious interesting and the complex understandable." I enjoy my work, sure, and most of the questions I receive are extraordinarily good, germane, challenging, and lead naturally to interesting columns. People are always surprised that the armadillo crosses a river by walking across the bottom, that the gnu can run so fast, that the marten is so small. Beyond the fun stuff—the "Where does 'playing 'possum' come from?" or "How are porcupines romantic?"—there are a lot of unanswerably weird letters about feathers and fur and the death of pets. I answer all my mail. I say "I don't know" sometimes in the letters. I have even answered all of the hate mail I've had in the last six months about the evolution problem, even though I use a photocopied form for those. It's not a surprise that I answer letters; Andy never wrote back to me.

The boys and I go to the airport to pick up my parents. Walking with my sons through the terminal is like magic for me, because I am a man with a secret. My parents are flying in from Michigan to stay with the boys for a week while Katie and I go to Hawaii. I'll have to spend one day with my old prof Sorenson in his research center at the university taking notes for an article on his first panda and then half of another at the Kapiolani Zoo, looking at their arrangements for the creature, but the rest of the time Katie and I will be having sexual intercourse with short breaks to eat. And I will figure a way to tell her I've been fired. This will be our first trip away from the boys, and as I noted, everybody is three. It has been like three years in space, the four of us in a capsule circling and circling in the dark. Every time there is a lull, someone floats by in your face. "Hi, Dad."

Katie and I moved our sex life later and later into the night, until it was being conducted with one of us half asleep, and then we tried the mornings, but the boys have always risen first and crawled in with us. Then we bought the VCR and used it to lure them into the living room mornings for twenty minutes of Chip and Dale cartoons while we touched very quietly in our bedroom and listened for little feet. That ploy actually worked pretty well for a while, and then we became guilty about using the TV that way.

We moved into the shower. That was always good, but it was difficult to hear in there and more than once we saw a small pink figure leaning against the frosted-glass shower doors. It was enough to take the starch out of things. Then a terrible thing happened: we became pragmatic about it. Interrupted once, we would shrug and smile at each other, rinse off, and start the day. Can I even explain how sad it made me to watch Katie pull on her clothing?

But now, I have a secret. I am one revolution of the earth away from the most astonishing sex carnival ever staged by two married people.

This is what I tell myself. And I believe it, but there's more. Though Katie hasn't said anything, I suspect she knows I'm not Zoo Lewis anymore. Cracroft told me I was history on Tuesday and then he's called and tried to be helpful twenty times. The syndicate is dropping the column. We both know why, but they cite numbers. I'm down to fifty-two papers from over a hundred and seventy. The papers are dropping the column. The *Blade*, the *Register*, the *Courier*, the *Post*. They can't handle the backlash. I'm too political. Maybe I am. It is no longer possible to write cute pieces about the dolphin, the mandrill, the Asian elephant. But this all started with four pieces on simple amphibians and what one of my hate-mail correspondents called "creeping evolutio-environmental liberal bullshit." Cracroft says *no problem*, most of the papers will do reruns of old columns for six months, and that should give me enough time to come up with some freelance stuff of a more "general nature" and maybe pitch a book.

Zoo Lewis bites the dust. Maybe he should. I was getting cranky. I've enjoyed it more than I planned to, and only one other time was there trouble: after I wrote an appreciation of the wolf, a very bright, misunderstood creature who mates for life. We got two pounds of mail from Montana and lost the *Star* and the *Ledger*.

Cracroft is a good guy. I don't blame Cracroft. He called and said I could keep my modem. He said, "I'm sorry, Lewis. Your work is good. It may just be time to shake up the feature page."

"What should I do?" I asked him. We've known each other for ten years.

"You're good," he said. "Go to plan B."

I smiled and thanked him for the modem. Plan B. Zoo Lewis *was* plan B. I was going to be a veterinarian. I was going to doctor animals, but I couldn't because of the allergies—they tried to kill me more than once. We can't even have a dog or a cat or a ferret. We can have fish in a tank, but I don't want fish. I couldn't be a vet, so I became a journalist. I'm in plan B. And it's not working.

At the gate, I am surprised. When my parents emerge, I have to look twice. It's not that I don't recognize them; it is that I recognize them too well. They haven't changed in a year. Why don't they look older? My mother wears her sure-of-herself grin, having gone out into the world once again and found herself still every bit the match for it. The interactions of men and women have always amused her. "Society," she used to tell me, "is not quite finished. Don't *ever* fret and stew about your place in it."

My father comes forward beside her, carrying his small valise in which there will be four or five pads of blue-lined graph paper already bearing the beginnings of several letters and drawings. He will have seen something from the window of the plane, where he always sits, that has struck him as worthy of improvement and he will have begun the plans. He works on half a dozen projects at a time. When he retired from General Motors four years ago, the grid pads just continued. He has fourteen obscure patents and is always working on two or three more in far-flung fields: a design for a safety fence for horse racing; a design for pressure tanks containing viscous liquids; a tennis racket grip. He writes me every week on the beautiful paper describing his projects and his current concerns. Most recently he's been considering the rules and statistics of baseball and has in mind several revisions. I watch my father approach with his easy stride and calm smile and I am paralyzed. He doesn't look older at all. He looks, and this has my mouth open, *just like me*. It took them almost forty years, but my genes have jelled. No wonder my three-year-old sons leap away, weaving through the travelers, to grab the hands of my mother and my father.

When I join them, my mother has already pulled two dinosaurs out of her bag and awarded one to each of the boys. I kiss my mother and when I step back she runs her hand up over my ear through the white in my hair and smiles. My father hugs me, letting his hand stay across my shoulder as he always has since my Little League days. Harry has examined his toy, feeling the snout and counting the claws, and finding it authentic, he is very pleased. "Isn't it great?" I say to him. "A brontosaurus."

"Dad," Harry corrects me. "It's not."

"It's an allosaurus," my mother says. I look at her and she gives me the look she's always had for me, the sweet, chiding challenge: *You can catch up if you'd like. None of this is beyond you.* But I'm not so sure. It may be beyond me, and if not, I'm not sure I want to catch up. It no longer surprises me that everyone is ahead of me. My parents are keeping up on dinosaurs.

At home, my father helps me start the barbecue and we stand on the patio in the early dark. He is drinking one of Katie's margaritas and looking around at the sky as if listening for something.

"We won't have a night like this until June," he says.

"I know. February is a bonus here. June is a hundred and ten." I am arranging the chicken pieces on the hot grill. I'd like to tell my father about what is happening, that my job is over, but there is really no need. He knows already. My mother let it slip on the phone that my column wasn't running in the *Journal* anymore. My parents have always been mind readers. He can tell that change is at hand by the way I use the tongs on the chicken. This mode of communication is actually a comfort. It spares our talking like people on television.

Years ago, I called home the night I knew I was leaving veterinarian school. I was in the hospital in Denver and when my mother answered she said, "It's your allergies, isn't it, Lewis? Are you in the hospital right now?"

Ricky comes out and loops an arm around my father's leg. "Granpa, Granpa, Granpa," he says and points at the chicken sizzling on the grill. "The barbecue is very hot. You must be very careful."

Ricky's head falls against my father's leg and as my father cups the little boy's head, I know how it feels. The two stand in that kind of hug and watch me as I begin to turn the chicken. This is who I am, some guy with a spatula at twilight. I write about animals. I won't get the big adventures, page-one stuff; I've stood on a lot of patios with my father and I'll stand on quite a few with my son. That is what I'll get.

Later, in our bedroom, Harry is helping Katie pack. She's got both big suitcases open on the floor and Harry sits in one with his binoculars. He's emptied my shaving kit and is sorting through the goodies. I reach down and try to find my razor. "I already put it on the bureau," Katie says. "Do you want your Hawaiian shirt?"

"What's the protocol? I don't think you take your Hawaiian shirt to Hawaii, do you?" It's a turquoise shirt with little red and white guitars and orchids printed all over it.

"If you don't take it, we may buy another."

"Take it," I say. "Let's take it."

Harry has pulled the lid down now and he's inside the suitcase. In twenty minutes, when my mother has taken Rick in to bed and read him a book and he's flopped over on his stomach aggressively for sleep, I will come back in here and find Harry asleep in my suitcase and carry him to bed.

Of course, when you have children, all your bedtimes come back to you. Not all at once, but from night to night, pieces of your earliest nights appear. It will be the sound of a sheet or the feel of a blanket and the dark in the corner or the way the light from the hall falls on the far wall and there you are being carried to bed by someone who must have been your father or there is your mother with her hand in your hair and your head on the pillow. Some nights I lie in their room with the kids and listen to their nursery-rhyme tapes and I listen to them as they swim in the sheets, Ricky diving down first into sleep, the same way he eats, hungrily, no sense wasting time, and Harry as he turns sideways on his back and then kicks the wall softly with his heels as his blinking grows longer and longer and then his eyes shut for good and I hear the motor of his breath even out in a perfect sine curve.

When Katie comes to bed it is just about midnight. I've been listening to some guy on Larry King's radio show talk about the economy. He keeps referring to the "quietude" of the nineties. He is advising people to keep gold under their mattresses. Katie hits the pillow with a blowout sigh, throwing her right arm up over her eyes. "Are we actually going on a trip?" she says. "Are we going to sleep for four days or what."

"Depends on what you mean."

She turns her head my way and smiles. "You monkey. 'The coast is clear.' " That's the line we've used for fifteen years. Petting in her front room, one or two o'clock in the morning, I was always whispering: "The coast is clear." Once on her dining-room floor as close to putting something on the permanent record as we'd ever been, everybody's pants to the knees, brains full of fire, we heard her father ten feet away in the kitchen drawing a glass of water. And now we'd been living like that again. It makes a person dizzy.

The length of her body is the simple answer to what I am missing. It's an odd sensation to have something in your arms and to still be yearning for it and you lie there and feel the yearning subside slowly as the actual woman rises along your neck, chest, legs. We are drifting against each other now. Sex is the raft, but sleep is the ocean and the waves are coming up. Katie's mouth is on my ear and her breath is plaintive and warm, a faint and rhythmic moan, and I pull her up so that I can press the tops of my feet into her arches. I run my hands along her bare back and down across her ribs and feel the two dimples in her hip and my only thought is the same thought I've had a thousand times: I don't remember this—I don't remember this at all. Katie sits up and places her warm legs on each side of me, her breasts falling forward in the motion, and as she lifts herself ever so slightly in a way that is the exact synonym for losing my breath, we see something.

There is a faint movement in our room, and Katie ducks back to my chest. There is someone in our doorway. It is a little guy without any clothes on. He has a pair of binoculars.

Who can remember sex? Who can call it to mind with the sensate vividness of actuality? I sit in the window when we lift off from Los Angeles. Katie sits in the middle and next to her a high school kid with a good blitz of pimples across his forehead. Katie speaks to him and I see he has braces. Beneath us I see the margin of the Pacific fall away. I can see all the way up to the Santa Monica Pier and the uneven white strip of sand separates the crawling blue sea from the brown urban grid of the city. We have just left something behind. We have now been released from mainland considerations. Tonight Harry is going to pad west in his bare feet, looking for us with his glasses, but the surf is going to stop him. He'll be mad for a moment at the Pacific Ocean, it's a big one, but then he'll turn and go back to his room.

I love to fly. I always sit in the window and press the corner of my forehead against the plastic glass. I can feel the little bumps in my skull which are full of ideas and I move my head slightly. It kind of hurts in a nice way. Today my skull is full of sex. I'm trying to remember sex. I don't even try to resist by making notes for Sorenson or looking at the magazine, *Inflight*. The fact that I have lost my job and may lose our house, the Buick, the VCR, seems to have sharpened everything, and I feel edgy, alive. The sun is clipping through my window and falls in a square on my wrists and lap. I hear the stewardess come by, her clothing whispering, and I glimpse her tight maroon skirt, seamless and perfect as it passes.

I've always loved to look at women, what is that, terrible? There are moments I harbor in memory: buying my first sport coat on my own downtown in Salt Lake City at Mednicks, the tall young woman helping me, taking the coat back to the counter and then bending down and writing the slips as her white silk blouse fell open like doors of a cathedral and her breasts were revealed to me hanging there in the cool dark, draped in white undergarments as delicate and complicated as certain music. Of course, it happens all the time. When I buy a boatload of groceries at Safeway, the girl asks for identification for my check and then she bends to check the name and numbers. Who would look away from this healthy and dextrous checker, her cleavage sweet as milk. It's as if once she has my driver's license and is certain of who I am, she feels free to show me her breasts. I think of it and it makes buying food magical. And there have been times more raw, when driving down the hot highways I would look down into the Chevelle next to me in the jam, cars from here to heaven, and see her, some weary brunette in a skirt, legs spread, one knee cocked against the door so that the air conditioning ran into the open maw along her bare leg all gooseflesh and pinfeather right into the damp crux of my imagination.

Now, in an airliner with my wife fallen into a book and the jolly boy next to her gnashing peanuts, I suck at a gin and tonic and roll my forehead against the window. Below it is all sea now, and I feel the sleepy discomfort of an erection or half an erection, some vaguely pleasant stretching, and I shift in my seat belt, and I smile. My face feels sleepy and stiff and the smile feels like some kind of little exercise. This is immaturity. This is total regression. I think. I'm half asleep and I'm remembering Ryan McBride.

When we finally got to high school, Rye and I found the information about sex vague and imprecise. We'd been promised in the rumor and legend of junior high something more explicit. We'd heard everything. We'd heard about girls fighting in the parking lot, one girl's bra used to choke her if not to death then into acute brain damage. We'd heard about "heavy petting," which is exactly the kind of phrase that made Rye spit with rage. "Oh, it's heavy," he'd say. "Which is the heavy part?"

We were a little ready to rip the veil off anything vaguely

masquerading as the unknown. We wanted to know. And it really got to Rye that people used the same phrases for everything.

"Doing it," they'd say. So-and-so were *doing it.*

"Totally bogus," Rye told me when we heard that about our old pal Paula Swinton and student body vice president Jeff Wild. "How could two words be more wrong? *Doing? Doing?"* he'd rant, his arms presenting the words to me in circles. "Doing?" He'd shake his head and say sadly, "It? Doing *it?* Paula and Jeff are doing *it?* What is it, one thing? Done one way? I mean, is it?" Rye would let his shoulders droop. Rye was a funny guy. He had a way, a campy way with his body. One shrug could get a room to laugh, and he'd been elected as student body secretary, the first boy ever to hold the office, on his reputation as a character. Standing there at his locker looking hurt in his green-and-gray class sweater, he mugged for me and went on, "Hey, Lewis, Lewis, Lewis. This is high school. This," he waved his book at the teeming corridor, "is secondary education." We started off for class and he put his arm over my shoulders and leaned on me. He whispered, "I had expected more. Paula and Jeff. *Please.* This place is letting me down."

And as an antidote for the ambiguity in which we floated, Rye became known, our junior and then senior year, as the guy who defined "heavy petting." "It's an ugly thing to see and if I were you I wouldn't look" was the first line of his credo as it appeared on blackboards and in graffiti in the stairwells. It closed: "It takes place below the waist." He said it as a student executive club meeting was breaking up, but it was noted on the blackboard in advanced English. In three weeks the phrase "takes place" could get a laugh in any sophomore class. A high school, we learned, is a three-story brick building with a jillion hormones and one trophy case.

He'd fall in step behind some junior in tight white Levi's, her rear bobbing like a searchlight, and he'd lean to me and say, "What is this feeling? The biological urge toward procreation of the species?" Then he'd elbow me and answer the question: "Nah."

His great and lasting fame derived, however, from planning the graduation party on Black Rock Beach and from his thesis: "Eleven," which postulated that there were eleven different kinds of erections. I can remember these things with a clarity that quiets me.

Katie has put her book on her lap and her head against my arm. It is sweetly warm here now, sunny with the kind of sleep that closes your eyes from the bottom up. The plane rides the white shell of air over the ocean, splitting silence into broomstraws, and I interlace my fingers carefully so as not to disturb my wife Katie. If you think I don't love her, you're not catching on. I close my eyes in the bright rushing world. I move my lips. So, what is this, more than it should be? I don't know. The truth: I'm praying.

The next: it doesn't last long. I move my lips carefully around the few important things I have to say and then use the bundle of my ten fingers to adjust the knob in my trousers. The walrus has a genuine bone in its penis that ranges in length between ten and twenty inches. The bone is an evolutionary device that is a great help in cold water. Eskimos save these bones, called "ooziks," for good luck. A sperm whale's penis, when erect, is nearly fifteen feet in length. The grizzly bear, more closely related to man, has erections that average four inches and require greater willing or unwilling cooperation from a mate. My watch tells me I've had this tumescence half an hour and at our speed that's three hundred and fifteen miles, a boner that could go from Denver—if I can hang on ten more minutes—to Santa Fe. It's the kind of erection Ryan used to call number three, the kind you get about ten in the morning in third period, a wonderful extension that makes you slide down in your seat and stretch your legs. It's related to number one, the one you wake up with, stiff as a clothespin. Number two was what? It was also a morning deal, the one that comes up between class, pointed down, trapped in your shorts pointing at five o'clock. Number two was the one you used your chemistry book to straighten out. What were the others? Eleven. We laughed our heads off, but we all knew he was right. There are eleven, minimum.

I remember the larky randiness of those days and my decision finally to push the point with a girl named Cheryl Lockwood at the graduation party. I wasn't really out of the mainstream in high school, most of our class were virgins, but I'd had a couple of relationships that had just dried up and blown away and I couldn't figure it out. I was a little worried, I remember, about being unqualified for the real world of men and women. Who doesn't? My parents, of course, could read my mind, but I could not read theirs. I lived in a kind of dread that my father would take me aside one evening or my mother would try to open the topic. As it was, we lived an uneasy truce. If we were watching television at night together and there was a kissing scene, I would always leave the room, glass of water, homework, something. I was out of there.

Cheryl Lockwood was a cutie. I wasn't going with Cheryl, a smart-looking girl with short brown hair and a nice bosom, but she was my chemistry partner, and whenever we talked, we flirted. Her favorite phrase was "What you going to do, huh? Huh?" It was all smile-smile stuff, but the undercurrent was there. The way we flirted was that I would tell her she had to put on some weight and she would moan about it, *oh, no, no,* like that, and then we'd light the Bunsen burner and melt something down. When I think of her I still smell sulfur.

My decision to make serious moves on her was a result of our being sent to the principal's office together for staining Mr. Welch's hands. Our teacher, Mr. Welch, of course, deserved it, because he understood chemistry and wasn't that willing or able to let the rest of us in on the secret. He was a terrible teacher. We did learn that sodium nitrate stains human skin, however, and we spread a thin layer on our counter just before asking him over to explain something about liquid sulfur. The next day his palms were gray and he sent me and then Cheryl (because she laughed) to the office.

On the way down there I was a little high, you know, from being kicked out of class and the halls were empty and there was Cheryl in step with me and we were kind of bumping together and I said, "There is something so sexy about empty hallways, don't you think?" I put my arm around her shoulder and she put her arm around my waist and squeezed, saying, "Absolutely. What are you going to do about it?" And I said, "I'm going to get you alone at the graduation party and have my way with you." She squeezed me tighter and said, "Good. I hope you enjoy it as much as I plan to." We met with Mr. Gonzalez, the principal, and he tried to be mad about what we had done to Mr. Welsh, but he had a little trouble.

And that was that. Cheryl and I didn't flirt for the last two weeks of school. I didn't try anything because I didn't want to break the spell. We had made some kind of deal that day in the hallway and we both knew it.

We land in Honolulu. I'm on the wrong side of the plane to see Waikiki, but I look down and see the water change, the seven layers of turquoise. When the wheels touch down, the plane bumps once in a soft, unreal way, and instead of thinking *we're really here,* I think: This seems unreal. And nothing that will happen for hours will dissuade me.

Our cab driver, for instance, is the same guy who took us to the airport in Phoenix. I lean back sleepily in the car and feel the strange air, moist and full of orchids and exhaust, and I see the back of his head. He must be working two shifts. He lets us off in the circular drive of the Royal Hawaiian and here the air wants to wake us, sweet with salt, in the dappled shady imbroglio of trees. I give the driver a big tip. He's going to need it to get back to Arizona by dawn. Here it is full afternoon, sunny but broken, and Katie stops me amid our suitcases on the steps of the hotel and kisses me. Just a little kiss. What am I going to do, make more of it than it is? No, some woman kisses you on an island.

When we register, there are two messages—one from Sorenson at the university, the other from Katie's friend from Tokyo, Mikki. While Katie makes the arrangement for our rental car, I step back from the majestic registration counter, smooth as marble and big as a boat. The wide Persian runners down the lobby's arcade are four inches thick. Down at the end through the glass atrium, I can see the lawn and a cluster of umbrellas around the bar, and further—through the palms—just a wedge of the fake blue sea. Katie takes my arm and says, "Let's go up and make our calls."

I smile as the boy bumps our old luggage into the elevator because I am thinking of Harry in my suitcase. He could be in there right now. You take your children everywhere.

I call Sorenson and he says to forget the zoo, to come directly to the university. He says to come *now* and gives me directions. In the tropical heat, I can feel my rash. Kate and I are in the room, fourth floor, and she has opened the shutters onto the beach and I can see a thousand bodies at their ease. The large catamaran nods in the sand in front of the hotel, its large green-and-white sail seems the flag of health. I ask a few questions, but Sorenson says, "We'll talk. I'll fill you in when you get up here." I can smell something wrong.

Katie has heard me on the phone. There is no need for us to talk. I'll be back later. "Are you okay?" I ask. "You're going to see Mikki?"

"I'll call her, meet her for a drink this afternoon."

It should be now that I bring it out—I lost my job—tell her. I can't do it. I'd end up defending something. I've still got six months' pay, residuals. She'd rail against the forces that have got me fired. I'd say something generous about the situation. I don't have it to be generous. Something crawled out of the sea two hundred million years ago, took a breath, and liked it. That guy has lost me my job.

I take a deep breath and then another, trying not to sigh, and take Katie's hand. "Let's kiss in front of the window," I say. "Be part of this place." When she comes to me in the sunlight, we kiss like two people in a movie, and I realize her arms are the reason I have a neck, an evolutionary device.

Then when I open my suitcase to grab a new shirt and find my powder, Harry's not in there. But the boys have left me a souvenir. I find the rental videocassette case and open it. *The Land of the Lost.* Harry's done a little packing for me. There's going to be a late fee on this classic.

At Sorenson's lab there's a little confusion. I take my bag and notes in our rental Toyota up the hill to the university and find his block building hidden among the million-year-old trees behind a little cemetery.

"The bear isn't here," he tells me.

"You moved it."

"No. It hasn't exactly arrived." Sorenson was one of my professors at Stanford and now, like everyone else, he's not getting any older. He's still got all his hair; he isn't any heavier; and he's still wearing the same wire-rims. It confuses me that I'm the same age as all these old guys. As always when things are working out, he seems unconcerned, peaceful. I think he was in physics before zoology, and he found out how fast the universe is expanding. It cooled him out about all the small stuff.

"Where is the panda, Phil?" I say. "Should we go see it?"

"There's a guy coming." He smiles. "He wants to meet Zoo Lewis."

I feel the plane ride humming in my sinuses. I sit on one of the metal stools. "There's a guy coming?"

"Right."

"Phil. Whose panda is this?"

Sorenson smiles and pours us each a cup of thick lab-
oratory coffee. I'm glad to be here even if he's being mys-
terious. He got me my first assistant editorship right after
I left veterinary school. He was the second one I called
from the hospital after the allergy attack, and like my
parents, he wasn't surprised.

Sorenson sips his coffee. "The Bible boys, did they get
you yet?" He grins. It's a great grin and it makes me grin
while I nod.

"They did."

"You started writing about the mammalian orders."

"The primates."

"Men are more closely related to tree sloths than are
squirrels."

"Not in some newspapers," I say. We're about to laugh.
"I lost the column. I'm going to do a piece on this panda
and then free-lance for a while. I'm going to plan C." It
feels good to level with someone. "The bad part is I had
one hundred and seventy-five papers; I was syndicated.
We bought a house."

"You've done some wonderful stuff, besides the newspaper deal," Sorenson says. "You can write anything you
want."

A Hawaiian kid comes in, dressed like we used to dress
in graduate school, a long-sleeved white oxford-cloth shirt,
khakis, white tennis shoes. "Mr. Sakakida is here," he tells
Sorenson.

"Ah," Sorenson says dramatically. "Mr. Sakakida. You're
on, Lewis. Good luck. Just go with Johnny."

The campus is as green as one of Rousseau's paintings
and quiet as a dream. The young people we pass all carry
books and whisper together. Johnny doesn't know who
Sakakida is, except that he is the person Sorenson has

been talking to on the phone for two months. Johnny calls him "the panda man." As we walk along it bothers me that I can identify so few of the trees, they all seem like ancient, outsize houseplants, grand and succulent, fit for dinosaurs. On a dirt path we cross through a shallow ravine, and in the thick shade we come up behind a huge pagoda.

"You can find the lab, right?" Johnny asks. He's stopped. He points off to his right. "It's just up there." He starts to move off. "Go around. The panda man should be out there."

There is a huge plum Mercedes with tinted windows parked on the gravel drive in front of the pagoda. As I start up the steps of the building, the passenger door of the Mercedes swings open and a tall oriental man in a gray suit steps out. He's wearing gold wire-rim sunglasses and he's smiling like mad.

"Dr. Wesley," he says with satisfaction.

"Mr. Sakakida?" I say and we shake hands and he bows. He waves at something in the shadows down the lane.

"We are very happy about this," he says. He's Japanese, his accent is clear. "We are glad an expert such as yourself is helping. We hope everything is fine. We are happy to help the people of Hawaii and the people of the United States of America." He bows again and goes back and steps into his car and closes the door and I watch it roll silently off through the trees.

I didn't even ask him a question. Before I can move, a new white Ford van appears and stops before me. Now I realize I can smell the cedar incense floating out of the pagoda. The driver of the van is all business. He's a large Hawaiian in a faded yellow Primo T-shirt. He wings open the van's rear doors and wants me to examine the contents.

In a slatted wooden crate there is a giant panda.

"Well," the guy says. "Are you taking delivery here?"

The bear isn't moving, and I crawl in the van. As soon as I do, I feel my pulse in my cheekbones; my face is swelling shut. She's alive—though I can tell by the overpowering smell and the matted hair that she's been in this box too long. There's hair everywhere.

"No," I say, and I can hear my allergies shutting my head down. "Drive me up the hill."

On the way back to the lab, my nose begins to run, voluminously. My face has begun to itch. My eyes are slits and I am breathing through my mouth. Allergies. That's okay by me; this is a giant panda. I feel the first excitement, but I can tell by my rasping breath that I am going to need a shot.

When we arrive at the lab, Sorenson and Johnny are ready. They've got the large cage prepared and all the equipment is clean and laid out. Sorenson takes the clipboard from my driver and then hands it to me. "You've got to sign," he says. "It'll be all right."

I sign the sheet and the driver leaves in the van.

"Heavens," Sorenson says to me. "Look at your face. Johnny, call Dr. Morris."

But when Sorenson sees the bear for the first time, he smiles. It may be dying, but it is something to see. His panda. Even my enthusiam is rekindled and when he asks me if I had any trouble, I simply say, "I met your Mr. Sakakida."

"But you're okay?" Sorenson says.

"I'm okay."

We sneak the panda in through his loading area on a gurney and start the procedures. She's shedding hair like an old doll. We take a pulse and draw blood and Sorenson and the kid start to clean her up. Old Sorenson can't get close enough. He's right in there, another phenomenon.

Ten minutes later, Dr. Morris arrives. He's a well-dressed Hawaiian with a beautiful black leather medical bag. He asks about my allergies, pries open my eyes to check my pupils, takes my blood pressure, and gives me two shots, a small one in the arm and a large one in the hip. By this time, Sorenson has finished the first set of procedures and shows Dr. Morris his prize, making the doctor promise not to tell anyone about the bear.

It's dark. I remember to call Katie. She's not in the room and I leave a message at the desk. There is still a lot to do tonight. We weigh the panda and Sorenson checks her nose, teeth, skin tone. He won't have the blood results until tomorrow, so I shake Sorenson's hand. We've all scrubbed and the panda is sleeping in her new cage.

"In a year, she'll have her own quad in the zoo."

"If she makes it through the night."

"Thanks, Lewis," he says. "I appreciate this."

"Who's Sakakida?" I ask.

"An importer."

"What's his real name?"

"I don't know."

"Yes you do." I stand up. "But you've got your bear." My rash now is a sharp itch. "And now I'm going to drive back to the hotel, and you will call me tomorrow so we can all go to a sumptuous dinner, your treat."

Sorenson comes to me at the door and takes my hand. "Lewis, she's going to thrive." He's high on having this animal here and his happiness makes me smile too. "You know it, Lewis. She's going to thrive."

I love his enthusiasm. I love old Sorenson really. He's been the author of so much of the good that's happened to me. As I drive back to the hotel, the world seems full of possibility again. All the lights are on in Waikiki, ten thousand hotel windows, and the streets swarm with parties of two, four, and six, polished and sunburned and looking for dinner.

At the Royal Hawaiian, I get out on the circular drive and give the keys to the attendant, who eyes me strangely. My face is still a little swollen and I smell like bear. I smell a lot like bear. It doesn't matter. In fact, it's wonderful. The hotel seems the very edifice of romance, glittering in the night, and I can hear drums. It's seven P.M. local time.

There is a phone message. The note reads: Dearest Lewis—I've gone with Mikki over to Kaneohe to see her parents. They leave tomorrow morning. Be back at ten or eleven. *The coast is clear*—wait and see. Love, K.

I thank the concierge and hand him back Katie's messages. I step back to the center of the lobby to read my note again. It's okay. It feels like a little present. I'm tired. I fold it into my pocket.

Going upstairs is a mistake. One person in a hotel room at this point in my life is a mistake. Especially with the drums: pum-pum-pum. But I quickly shower and powder up my rash, which is slightly bigger and real angry. I dress in a pair of light khakis with my sandals and Hawaiian shirt. But I can't go out the door with that shirt on. It's too nutty. My head is almost back to normal. There are some splotches of red, but the swelling has subsided. But this shirt. So I throw a blue blazer over it and look pretty good—like the ne'er-do-well son of the local gentry.

In the elevator, I'm thinking of a riddle Ricky asked me last week: Why did the young pencil call "Yoo hoo"? Answer: Because his mommy was in the forest. It suddenly makes perfect sense to me. His mommy was in the forest. I need a drink. I'll have a civilized cocktail and Katie will come back.

From the lobby, when I open the door, the drums blast me, sucking up all the air. Boom. Boom-boom. Boom. Boom-boom. Boom. Two big drums like that in the torchlight. There are, I notice immediately, no little drums. No tambourines. No maracas. Two big drums. Boom. Boom. Boom. Boom. It makes you duck, this noise. I walk to the cabana in step, boom—boom—boom—boom, leaning against the percussion, in fact, and grab on to the bar. I can feel the drums in my chest against the wood.

Behind me under the torchlight on the lawn, the island dance show is full swing. Six big guys in leafy skirts are stomping up and down and juggling torches. It's a big show, everything's big. There are no small guys. Then the women come out and they're big too. The bartender, another guy in a Hawaiian shirt and a pencil behind his ear, is at my elbow and I order a mai tai. The women are doing something I can only describe as the hula and their hips are winging in astounding figure eights. Their movement is mesmerizing. It is something one should call a feat. I stare at the woman nearest me and all I can do is wonder at the axle of her pelvis, how it could bear such radical and smooth leverage.

The little bar patio is only half full, so I take my drink over to one of the perimeter tables and sip the rum. There is a purple blossom in my drink as well, which I eat. I watch as the women vibrate double-time for a couple of minutes and then promenade off. Everyone applauds, even the people across the lawn inside the luau room. Next to me two young women in sleeveless summer dresses are drinking large red drinks, and on their table is a line of six little drink umbrellas and a little bouquet of wet orchids. Two lawyers from Houston is my guess. "Is that something, or what?" one of the women says to me. I smile and nod. The torchlight flares unevenly and I think I need more torches in my life. More torches and more ocean and more beaches. I can feel the pressures in my head shifting. The cocktail waitress in her green sarong slips by and I order another mai tai.

It was Ryan McBride's idea to have the graduation party at Black Rock Beach on the Great Salt Lake. It was a weird idea, because in those days the Great Salt Lake was different than it is today. In the old days it was a strange and superlative place. It was the saltiest body of water on earth. It was saltier than the Dead Sea and it was six times saltier than the ocean. It was famous for salt. The mineral content was so high that bathers bobbed like corks on the surface and there were several famous postcards that showed five or six people sitting in the water as if on easy chairs. Through several years the Great Salt Lake, which was hundreds of square miles, was as salty as water can get. In twelfth-grade chemistry, before things got bad, we had studied the way salt would precipitate up an anchor rope, climbing like frost two or three feet above the surface of the water.

The lake itself sat in the broad desolate alkali desert dish twenty miles west of Salt Lake. There were few amenities, just an access road which left tourists on the half-mile-wide beach among the swarming brine flies. At Black Rock Beach there was a magnificent wooden pier which stood like a ruin high and dry, hundreds of yards from the then receding waters of the great salty lake. From time to time, some misguided soul would set up his hot dog stand near the pier and lose money all summer long.

Years before, of course, in the thirties and forties, the water had been high and there had been a famous resort on the water: Saltair, where trainloads of citizens could spend the day riding rides, bobbing in the water, and then dancing until after midnight. It had been abandoned and burned down before I was born. But when we graduated from high school the shores of the Great Salt Lake were the most forbidding place I'd ever seen on this planet. It was a vast, treeless, forlorn place smelling of brine, and even as my classmates began to park their shiny cars on that shore and climb out in their graduation clothes, bright and new and calling to each other in the twilight, it could have doubled for a tragic Martian landscape peopled by teenagers from Earth.

Cheryl Lockwood had written in my yearbook, under her picture in the Ski Club: ". . . And what are you going to do about it? Love and *expectations*, Cheryl." Something major was going to happen, I could tell, and I took her aside at the yearbook-signing party the night before graduation, placing my hand way up under her arm and marching her outside the gym and all the way to the thirty-yard line on the football field where, I'll say, I kissed her, but in fact I started to talk to her, saying only, "Meet me at the party tomorrow, and come alone." Whereupon she kissed me and then we twisted closer and kissed again like two doomed lovers under the five-story backside of our high school looming above us, the clock's ponderous lighted face tragic and remote and, as always, six hours ahead.

Graduation day was graduation day, of course, elevated and strange, perceived primarily in the stomach, I remember, as I must have been too sober for her tastes, because over lunch, which I ate alone in our empty kitchen in a house that was already seeming someone else's, my mother sat down with me for just a minute and said, "Oh my, the last sad meal at home for the Porcupine." (Union's symbol was the Porcupine.) "And tuna fish at that. Graduation is such sweet sorrow, Lewis," she went on, "but I want you to know that even after you graduate and you begin to wrestle with life's big problems ..." She was grinning in her omniscient way.

"Mom, I'm eating here, okay? Could we maybe talk later?"

She was having a wonderful time, but I was sweating that maybe she knew somehow that I'd been dreaming about the way Cheryl Lockwood had felt against my chest and planning the way things were going to go tonight late at the Great Salt Lake. After years of living in dank and cloudy ambiguity, I was going to find something out tonight with Cheryl. Promises had been made. We were going to *do it*. And here I was with my mother. I held my sandwich to my face like a veil.

"Lewis, Lewis," she said. "You're on your way and tomorrow you'll be out in the real world." She stood and came around the table, casually checking my forehead for fever. "But I'll still be your mama." She laughed softly. "Remember that," she said and went off to other errands.

That afternoon Rye picked me up in his huge Oldsmobile as always, but it was utterly different. We went to

Ketchum's Lumber and filled the trunk with a load of free warped odd bits for the bonfire and then we cruised west on the old highway, which was rippled with ten thousand tar patches. Three carloads of classmates met us at Black Rock Beach in the afternoon sunlight and after we'd dumped all the wood, Rye stepped back and took it all in. "This, my friends, is *serious*," he said. At first we all thought he was speaking about the ugly pile of wood, but then he spread his arms to take in the wasteland. "Congratulations on your impending graduation from high school in America. Your first responsibilities as graduates will be to meet me here right after dark for an extended pagan ritual." He nodded sagely and rolled his eyes. "Bring a date."

It was probably out there on the sour ragged edge of the saltiest lake on earth that I felt the rules change. I was watching Ryan entertain the troops for a minute before we climbed back in his car and headed for town and graduation. I remember looking back at the city spread on the mountains twenty miles away. There was still a good amount of snow on the peaks, even in June, and the houses on the hills looked like the remnants of someone else's life. Oh, the feeling was enough to close my callow throat, scary and delicious.

On the way back to town, I wanted to talk. I wanted to ask Ryan, whom I had known for years, if he felt it too. But we didn't talk that way. There had been lots of times that spring as I climbed in the old Oldsmobile when I'd wanted to say, "These are the electric nights, right? Can you feel it? What is going on?" We were seniors on the baseball team, and State Street had been granted to us, the new kings. We went out almost every night in Ryan's car that spring, and the nights were just full, the way May can pack a night when you're seventeen, which is so different from being sixteen. The nights were sweet and long and then suddenly, after cruising State and grabbing a cheeseburger at the Breeze Inn and maybe a Coke for the road, I was being dropped off in the new cool dark and even my old house looked beautiful to me too. Oh god, what nights. Something was going to happen, but I didn't know what it was, and I took the not knowing as my just being seventeen.

The drums stop. The air descends in a hum and I look up and see the dancers rearranging themselves for the torch dance. The patio is now full and two young couples are standing behind my table watching the show. The men have navy haircuts and wear new Hawaiian shirts. The drummers are moving their drums to each side of the raised platform now, and I take it as a cue and stand up, offering the honeymooners my table.

"I've been sitting too long," I say, waving them in. It's the truth: my rash is at me like fire ants and I'm happy to stand and shake things out. When I turn for the waitress, one of the women at the next table catches my eye and motions me to a chair.

"You can sit with us," she says. "This is a good part. We saw it last night." So I sit down with the two women and have another mai tai, which I know is in the margins of my limit, because I've just decided it is the best drink possible and I plan to drink them always and always.

I'm wrong about the women, I can tell immediately. They're not from Houston and they're not lawyers. By the stack of wrecked umbrellas and orchids I can only tell that they've each had four of the large red drinks. They are in their early thirties and both wear wedding rings. Before I can properly introduce myself or find out exactly who they are, the drums explode again, and so we all smile at each other and watch the show.

I haven't seen the torch dance for a long time, but it only takes a moment for me to decide that it is my favorite dance in the history of dance and I'm going to watch it every chance I get. It's the one where the big guy comes out and sits on the flaming barrel. He's wearing a huge leaf skirt, made of real leaves with some kind of oil on them that prevents them from burning, and he sits on the flames with the drums beating and then he rises and the flames shoot right back out again and then he sits down a little longer on the flames and then he finally gets up and the flames still flare and then with the bom-bom-bom of the drums he stands at the edge of the platform, smoke rising from his skirt and sweat shimmering across his forehead.

I can feel myself sweating, and the woman nearer to me says as a kind of whisper, "Don't do it again." She's talking to him, but the dancer moves back behind the flaming barrel and this time kind of attacks it, hopping up and sitting down securely on the flames, looking left and right. The woman next to me says now, "Get up. Oh, get up." It is real concern. As I hear it I recognize the midwest in her voice. Indiana. We exchange looks and raise our eyebrows and then turn back to the stage, where, after another fifteen seconds, the man jumps off the incinerator and reveals that he has put out the flames. The crowd applauds like crazy, clapping and clapping. There is great relief in this ovation. The show is over. The man takes a deep bow, and a large white smoke cloud rises from his skirt.

"Where on earth would they dream up a dance like that?" the woman across from me says.

"You guys are sisters, aren't you?" I say.

"Yvonne," says the one next to me, putting her hand on her chest. She's younger than her sister and her hair is lighter. "And this is Clare."

"I'm Lewis," I say. "And you are both from Indiana."

"Iowa," Yvonne says. "Dubuque."

"And you're here doing research on native dances."

"We're on vacation," Clare says. "We're on a two-week vacation from winter." She's a severe and pretty woman who looks a little starved. Her attention is given to the two couples at the next table.

"And are you on vacation?" Yvonne asks me.

"Yes," I say. "I'm doing a little work, but mainly my wife and I are on our first vacation from the kids."

The hotel's combo has set up in the gazebo and has begun playing. I signal the waitress again and order us all another drink.

"Is she here?" Yvonne asks.

"No. Not yet. She's off seeing friends tonight."

When the drinks arrive, the women take a moment to drain their old ones and then hand the glasses to the waitress. Simultaneously, they withdraw the little umbrellas from the daiquiris and line them up with the others. Our table looks like a miniature Shanghai street scene. I raise my glass. "A toast I've never ever made before," I say. "To Dubuque."

Yvonne touches my glass, but Clare is lost to the newlyweds. "Clare?" I say, motioning with my glass. She looks at me blankly and then her face ripples and dissolves. She's crying. She's folded her face into her hands and is crying over her big red drink.

I look to Yvonne: "Oh, my god. I'm sorry . . ."

"Let's dance," Yvonne says, and she's lifted me away from the table. The band is playing a series of Elton John's greatest hits, right now it's "Daniel," and Yvonne and I bumble into a loose embrace at the edge of the group of dancers and she tells me the story. The sisters are both widows. Their husbands, two brothers, were killed in a grain-elevator explosion in May. It has been a terrible time, especially for Clare. "You can understand," Yvonne tells me as the song ends. "She can't shake it. It's right here." Yvonne holds her hand in front of her face. "I'm going to be okay, but Clare, Clare is still hurting."

As she gives me all this news, I feel my buzz change. The high drunken feeling from the mai tais shifts now, and though I know I'm still mildly drunk because I think Elton John is the greatest musician that ever lived and I make a plan to listen to him all the time when we get home, I feel heavier, more controlled. I check my watch: ten minutes after eleven.

"I'll dance with her," I tell Yvonne.

"You could try."

Back at our table, Clare has finished crying and is sipping her drink through the straw while she watches the foursome next door come back from dancing. They bump into chairs and laugh. I sit and extend my forearms onto the table as if I had big news. "Listen," I say, "Do you guys know the difference between a diplodocus and an allosaurus?"

Yvonne's being a good sport and shakes her head no, but Clare gives me that flat, open-eyed look that means she's going to cry again.

"Clare," I say too loudly. "Shall we dance?"

Yvonne stands and helps Clare scoot around. Now the

band is presenting a middle-of-the-road version of "Your Song," and when I take Clare into my arms, I feel her stiffen. Out of the corner of my eye I can see the corner of her eye, and the way we are arranged it feels like close combat, like dancing with your enemy.

There are times in my life, perhaps too many times, when I feel utterly unqualified for the present moment. I had that feeling when I looked up from the examination table in veterinary school and saw the faces of my classmates looking at my ballooning face as I wheezed once and passed out. I feel this way now with Clare when the song ends and we haven't said word one and I am very ready to get back to my mai tai, the greatest drink on the island, but she doesn't move. She doesn't take her arm from my shoulder or her other from my hand. She stands stock still. I do too. There are other couples milling, embracing, so we're not really a spectacle, but the heat rises in my face anyway and I think: Of course, this is perfect. An unemployed journalist from Arizona who has been up for twenty hours is dancing on the patio of the Royal Hawaiian Hotel with a young widow from Dubuque. What will you do now?

The band kicks into a slow jazz number and Clare starts to lead. She's a good dancer, really, steady and right on the music. I pull back for a moment and say, "You know what I do? I work with pandas." She gives me a scary appraising look and I add, "Panda bears. I was a writer."

"That's okay," she says. "You'll be okay."

But when we fall together after that interchange, the whole dynamic scatters. Clare adjusts herself, hitching her arm around my neck further, and drawing her body against mine.

"Vonnie told you about Frank and Allen, didn't she."

"Yes," I say. Clare grips me at the neck. We won't be talking anymore. I can feel her against me like a drumbeat and I simply dance. Slowly. It is one of the closest embraces I have ever engaged in in public. She is pulled up so that our ears are almost touching and I can feel—with every step—the lean hardness of her body. The keyboard player is leading the combo through "Feelings" now, milking the vacant maudlin song to the limit. I look over and see Yvonne at our table and she gives me a brave nod: *Good for you, keep it up.* Clare and I have tightened things right up and now I can feel her pubic bone bruising against me with every move, intentionally, but I don't give way. She's using it to search my pelvis the way an impatient woman roots her purse for keys, and then she's found it, and hungrily she stays right on the beam. The other dancers seem oblivious to our humping; this is the age of dirty dancing or whatever, so I close my eyes and follow as she tilts frankly into me, pressuring me up to nine o'clock and then quickly to eleven. This would be the right time for Katie to show up, of course, and I could explain how I was comforting the sisters. The other couples have fallen into two-armed embraces, but Clare and I keep our clasped hands out in a classic ballroom pose, perhaps a trifle low, while our hips work like two guys tunneling out of prison.

My father told me a few things about sex. A person remembers these scenes. It was one of those nights when I was going out and I was reading *Time* magazine in the living room waiting for Ryan to honk. My father always wore plaid shirts after work with the sleeves rolled and his pencils in the pocket. He was a practical man who everywhere he went had a pencil, and though I may be more reticent than he is mostly, I am just like him with that pencil. He was an engineer and he took that approach.

"Let's talk about sex for a minute," he said. I remember he didn't say "What do you know about sex?" or "What do you want to know about sex?" No, we were in this together. We were going to talk about sex for a moment. "I'm sure that you understand the technical principles involved," he said. "The guiding physical laws of sexual intercourse between a man and a woman are very simple. You know how the man is designed, and a woman is constructed in a complementary fashion in terms of the location of the vagina and its angle. These things are obvious. What isn't as obvious to students of anatomy and sex is another essential principle of engineering." Here he asked a question: "Do you know what that principle is?"

"No, sir, I don't."

"That principle is *cooperation*. These things are all designed to facilitate sexual intercourse, but without the element of cooperation, it won't work the way it is intended. The results will be all wrong. Cooperation is the most complex concept about sex. You're going to hear a lot about love and responsibility in the next few years. Just remember they are simply part of this idea of cooperation." He stood up. "This isn't a great talk, but it's ten times what any of your pals are going to get from their dads. You'll be all right. There's no hurry."

Ryan McBride had another approach. He was still a virgin too, but when he heard that Cheryl Lockwood was meeting me at the party, he became all wisdom. "You want something to happen, right?" he told me on the way to the party graduation night. I was floating in a new freedom, still seeing myself cross the podium an hour before to pick up my diploma. I marched down the aisle, where my father stepped out and put his arm around me. He was stuffing his paper and pencil into his jacket pocket, for he had designed yet another thing—a more efficient way of distributing the diplomas without losing the sense of ceremony. His arm still around my shoulder, we walked outside the gym, where my mother in a pretty blue silk dress was waiting under the leafy campus sycamores. He and Mom were going out to dinner, and Mom smiled and said, "Welcome to the real world, where tomorrow morning bright and early we're going to weed the garden. So don't stay out too late." She kissed me on the cheek and added, "Congratulations."

Then I was in the Oldsmobile with Ryan, both of us jerking around changing clothes as he drove around the west side, picking up the big boxes of hot dogs, the bags of buns, the eight cases of soda, and the three cases of Coors from his uncle's garage, and then striking out on the old highway toward the lake. It was like rocket travel, our ship breaking clear of civilization, and slipping further and further into the wasteland void, carrying enough hot dogs for the rest of our lives. The sun had set and it was June: the earth glowed beneath us. Ryan was hollering theory. "If," Ryan pounded his right hand into the seat between us, "you want something to happen tonight with Cheryl, then you need to be realistic about how it would happen, and you know," he was growing gradually louder, beating the seat with each phrase, "that you are not going to do anything. Do you hear me? You know and I know that you are not going to do anything. You are not going to make one move. So. Listen to me. The secret is: let things *get out of control!*" I reached over and righted the steering wheel so we moved back onto the paved roadway. "So listen. Just do this. Horse around." He saw my face and said, "That's right, just horse around. Dance, bump, push, shove, touch, touch, touch. Horse around until you can let her know . . . that you're aroused. That's all it takes." Ryan had stopped pounding now and he had both hands on the wheel, but he was emphasizing his theme by turning to me after every sentence and squinting. "Once a girl feels she has aroused you, she's obligated. Girls are responsible people. They're not like guys. If they feel they've caused something, they take care of it." I squinted back at him and nodded, but I was full of questions, wondering if what he said was true and wondering—if push actually came to shove that night with Cheryl—what I would do.

In the middle of the next dance, Clare and I turn so I can see our table through the other dancers and I see something odd. Yvonne is talking to a pretty dark-haired woman whom I recognize as Katie. My wife is sitting with Yvonne and they are talking like classmates, and then Yvonne points at us and Katie looks, catches my eye, and waves. Clare and I are still slow-dancing, ignoring the rock beat of "Jambalaya," locked together in a pelvic clinch that has me up under the waistband of my undershorts, pain and pleasure, while she bumps and clings, her pubic bone like a blade cutting a new road in the wilderness as she breathes short and sharp against my neck. Around us the dancers are twisting and hopping, and we must look oddly stationary to my wife. I smile and nod at Katie, lift my hand from Clare's back and waggle a short wave, but as I do I feel Clare grip me as if I was going to drop her out a window and I hear air in her teeth once, twice, and she rises against me softly now and falls, and then the grip is gone and she is floating loosely in my arms. She relaxes and pulls back and when I look in her face she is contorting and rolling her eyes, clearing them the way people do who wear contact lenses, her forehead corrugating. Finally she sees me watching her. "What?" she says, averting her face. "So, what do you do with pandas."

At the table Yvonne stands and says to Katie, "This is my sister, Clare." Katie shakes her hand and we all sit down.

"We've been dancing," I say. "You missed the torch dancers." The waitress appears and busily clears the table, deftly setting a glass of wine in front of Katie. I see the other women aren't having any more. As I settle in my chair my rash flares.

"We've had a nice talk," Yvonne says to me.

"How long have you been married?" Clare asks.

"Fourteen years."

"That's wonderful," Clare says. She smiles at me. She's being sincere. "That is really wonderful." When she stands, she seems very tall. She goes on, "Well, Vonnie, I don't know about you, but this farm girl is up too late."

The sisters depart, each giving me a handshake out of a business manual, Yvonne clasping my hand in both of hers and saying, "You've been so kind."

For a moment I consider beginning an explanation, but it would start, "Their husbands . . ." and I let it go. I feel a simple relief at being alive and I just smile at Katie.

We aren't fully out of the lift when I take Katie in my arms and we kiss. "This is great," she says, as we amble down the carpeted hall in a four-legged embrace, turning, and pressing into each other. "This is hungry kissing, do you know that? Remember?" She's up against me again, her arms cinch. "Hungry kissing?"

We undress before we remember to close the door, I'm not kidding, and then in the bed, she rolls a naked leg onto me and I tell her the story of the day, not telling her about Dr. Morris and his shots. The whole time I'm telling the tale, we're moving with each other and from time to time she reaches down and checks the progress of this erection, the twelfth kind, and when she does that our moving rechecks itself and changes gear. This is what storytelling should be, this is the kind of attention narrative desires.

I bring the day right up to the torch dance and stop. Katie pulls me over onto her now and says, "You know, I've never seen you dance before. I've never seen you dance with another woman."

Now this next part, the bodies roll, their design made manifest, and there is achieved a radical connection. I'm not talking about souls. Who can tell about this stuff? Not me. You're there, you are both in something, something carnal and vaporish at once. Your mouths cock half a turn and you sense the total lock. You're transferring brains here; your spine glows. You go to heaven and right through, there's no stopping. What do you call it? Fucking? Not quite right here, this original touch, the firmament. My credo: you enter and she takes you in. This is personal. This is cooperation. Who can live to tell about it? You cooperate until you're married cell to cell, until all words flash away in the dark.

We roll apart, seizing onto our pillows as if they were life preservers. After a moment, Katie places the backs of her fingers on my cheek. She says, "I've got to go to sleep."

She smiles and her eyes close. "Don't worry about the column. You don't need it. You're a writer. There are a million things to do."

Mornings, many early mornings, the boys will climb onto our bed—how many times have I been bounced awake?—and either sit on my head and talk to Katie or fish from the foot, casting my robe sash into the icy waters beneath us. They have phenomenal luck always, hoisting dozens of large fish, reptiles, and other treasures from the sea and immediately offering them to us to eat. I lie there as Ricky wedges a piece of graham cracker in my mouth, saying, "Have some fish, Dad. Really. These are good." Katie is sanguine about all this as she sits in the pillows and asks Ricky for a little lemon with her fish and Ricky pantomimes the lemon. Harry keeps a lookout on the prow, his inverted binoculars showing the doorway out there somewhere on the edge of the lost world.

If I don't eat my fish right away, Katie says to me, "Hey, Dad, get with the program. These guys are fishermen. Come on. It's better than being nomadic wanderers." What can I say? It is one of mankind's oldest struggles: life on a boat. Two guys want to fish in the open air. One guy wants to feel his wife's bare thigh under the warm covers and fish later.

Now in our bed in the Royal Hawaiian Hotel, I can feel my wife descending in sleep. I can almost feel her falling away into night. She goes deeper with every breath. But I am full of allergy medicine and mai tais. I swing my legs out of bed and go to the window. Things are quiet all along the shore.

On Black Rock Beach twenty years ago I thought I was going to blunder across one if not all of the sexual frontiers. The scene was set, and I was ready. Night came on like the first night on earth, the sunset blistering the surface of the Great Salt Lake with the same wincing flash that it spread across the west desert sky, a flare that took our eyes and then chilled in a minute, replaced by the charcoal shadow of the planet.

Ryan lit the gas-soaked pile of lumber with a paper rolled in a ribbon which he told everyone was his diploma, and our little fire ripped into the dark. We had four sawhorse tables of food and drinks, and some guys had set up two large speakers in the back of a pickup and the flat sandy wilderness rang with Bobby Vee, the Four Seasons, Del Shannon, the Beatles, Dick and DeeDee, Roy Orbison, the Coasters, Johnny Mathis, the Boxtops, Richie Valens, the Shirelles, Andy Williams, Dion, and occasionally some wise guy would slip in Gene Autry or the Mormon Tabernacle Choir. Ryan kept the beer in the open trunk of his Olds. I remember how beautiful and illicit it looked in there, a tub of gold cans in silver ice. I thought: This is it, we're going to drink beer. I'd had a few, most of them with my father on the days when we'd poured the patio or leveled the yard, but this was different, this was a tub of gold cans on silver ice at the edge of the known world.

It was a hundred teenagers goofing around and dancing in the perimeter of a small fire by the wide margin of a big lake. And though we had miles of open space, no one wandered far from the fire. A couple might go for a walk, but there was something about knowing that there was *nothing* down that beach, nothing along the five hundred miles of coastline, not a thing, that sent them back quickly to the circle of light.

For the first hour, I manned the barbecue, blackening the hot dogs just right and then stacking them to one side of the grill. This was the real world, I remembered. Hot dogs were a hard sell. I saw Cheryl Lockwood as soon as she arrived with three other girls. Many of the girls, including Cheryl, wore their white graduation dresses and they stood in the firelight like princesses, their beauty heightened by the raw, malodorous kingdom. When they danced, and I watched Cheryl dance with a series of my friends, it was confounding that such untouchable womanhood could surf, pony, jerk. One by one they retreated to cars and changed into bermudas or Levi's and returned as the girls we knew, and the dancing became even more animated, even in the sand, as "Runaround Sue" beat into the night.

Not long after she returned in a pair of cutoff Levi's and a red football jersey, Cheryl came over to the grill. I saw she had a beer in her hand. She poked at the black papery skin of the hot dogs, finally pinching one and picking it up and examining it. "Do I dare? Who's the cook around here?"

I looked at her: "Dare."

"Dare *you*. You gonna cook all night?"

"No, Ryan'll be here in a minute."

"Good," she said and she leaned over and kissed me lightly. "Good. Then what you gonna do?" She smiled and walked back to the dancers.

I could see my old friends Georgia Morris and Paula Swinton. Paula leaned against the handsome Jeff Wild with whom she was supposedly "doing it," and Georgia had been going with an older guy for two years. He was twenty-five or something. Those girls didn't even know who I was anymore.

Ryan finally emerged from the tangle of parked cars where he had been goofing off with most of the baseball team. They were into the beer real good, and he brought me a can.

"You're a good guy," he said, trading it for the spatula. "Good luck."

I took my beer and walked off a little ways and then I walked way out, down the beach four hundred yards. No one was out there. I wanted to see it all for a moment, the party. I cracked the beer and took a sip. The firelight in everybody's hair and off the corners of the cars made it look like a little village in a big dark void. The dimensions were all vast. I seemed real small. I always seemed real small. I started to walk back. In a world so indifferent and illimitable, it was time to horse around with Cheryl Lockwood.

I found her sitting on the hood of a car, and we danced ten dances in a row, fast and slow. She was looking at me every time I looked at her. During the slow dances I bumped her when I could and tried to let her know that I dared. It was when we went back behind the cars to grab another beer that we started kissing. She guided me around and onto the trunk of someone's Thunderbird and we grappled there for half an hour or so, until we'd exhausted the possibilities of such a place. I had her bra undone, a loose holster in her shirt, and she had both hands in my back pockets.

It was then that she whispered, "Let's go swimming." When we stood, I was kind of dizzy, but we wended among all the cars and then we sprinted down the beach faster than I'd ever run before. Half a mile from the party, we stopped and kissed again, starting right in all over, but she pulled away and simply took off her clothing. I could barely hear "The Duke of Earl" across the sand, and then I stripped and headed out for the water hand in hand with Cheryl. It was an extraordinarily shallow lake and it took us a long time to get knee deep. When we did, she came against my naked body and I felt the contours of a naked woman for the first time. Behind her I could see the supine form of Antelope Island lying like an alligator five miles away. Then she turned and pulled me deeper in the water, saying something odd, something I've never forgotten. "Lewis," she said, her voice naked too, "I'm giving you the big green light."

And that was what I was thinking of—that this is really it: we were going all the way—when the water rose up my thighs and in a sudden dip, the warm water washed over my genitals and we were in up to our waists. Cheryl let go of my hand and sat backward in the sea, bobbing back up, arms, breasts, knees, and thighs. It was quite a vision.

It took about three seconds for me to realize what was happening and I felt it first as an odd spasm of chill up my back and then as a flash of heat across my forehead and sweat and then the final thing, the real thing, as the salt bit into my crotch like acid. There was no air. The pain rose way over my head like smoke. My jock rash was almost ninety square inches of raw skin counting both legs and my scrotum. The pain was like no pain. It was a quick unrelenting pressure on my temples, and I went out.

I lost the next five minutes, but whatever happened I give a lot of credit to a naked seventeen-year-old virgin named Cheryl Lockwood, who floated me back to the shallows where I woke looking into her face. I can still summon a brief glimpse of the outline of her breasts in the starlight as I spat salt water and tried to recover. So she saved my life, but I further credit her with saving the last slivers of my ego by not commenting on what had happened. She could so easily have said a dozen things about what this guy did when confronted with the big green light. When I sat up, the pain had become a real thing, a flaring heartbeat in my balls, that had me breathing through my teeth all the way back to the party. Our wet hair and damp clothing were huge hits at the bonfire, but because it was late and there had been worse behavior by others, it was bearable. Later, much later, when everyone was gone and Ryan and I threw the larger bits of debris into his trunk, I told him the truth: I'd failed.

"It means nothing," he told me and then he went on in a way that reminded me of why he was my best friend. "You went out after dark and passed out in the Great Salt Lake. Come on, who can do that?"

It's much later into the night and I'm in the beautiful men's room off the lobby of the Royal Hawaiian Hotel washing my hands and singing Roy Orbison's "Crying" at about six on the ten scale and it sounds pretty good. The walls are black marble in which you can see your shadow and they polish the song so that it reverberates mournfully. This is, without doubt, the best song I've ever heard.

Although Katie has parachuted into sleep, the day won't abandon me, and I have toured the grounds, walked up to the Outrigger for a drink, and returned to the hotel for a nightcap before coming in here. It is just a minute after two A.M.

> That I'd been cry-i-ing
> O-ver you . . ."

A big Hawaiian guy comes in and stands at the urinal, but I can't stop myself. I'm drying my hands and I must finish the song: the killer rhyme of *understand* and *touch of your hand* before all the "cry-ings". The guy stands at the sink and I recognize him as the torch dancer, my hero. He washes his hands with gusto and does the last few "cry-ings" with me. When we stop, I am as sad as I've been in ten years. All animals are sad after sex. This is a magnificent men's room. Our reflections stand ten feet deep in the marble like two sad visitors from the dead. The man points at me fraternally and says with great conviction: "Roy Orbison was a giant." He leaves.

My Hawaiian shirt is limp with sweat and I look like a guy who is just a little old to be a playboy. I consider doing "Only the Lonely," but it's clear that I do not have the stamina. I haul my sport coat straight and walk back out into the night. The bar is empty now, the bartender stands talking on the telephone, folding the last bar towel. I walk past the cabana through the little garden and down the cement steps to the beach. The light here is weird, the sand glowing and the sea simply a slick black space. Down along Waikiki, the hotels glimmer like ships awaiting departure. I pass the large catamaran.

"Dancing with the widows," I say aloud. I'm not really drunk anymore, but I'm still unmoored enough to talk out loud. I'm through singing, I think. Two women whose husbands have been blown to ashes. I picture it, a warm still spring afternoon, the air full and quiet, one brother sweeping the cement floor of the empty tower, the other straightening a bent hinge in the metal door when the dust trembled and fused and it all blew. The air turning white in a dust flash as big as the town had ever seen, thumping the sides of things for two miles, and afterward only the smoking hole, a few chunks of concrete coming down six blocks away, the one brother's pickup cartwheeling across the rail spur, blown like a wind-twisted section of the sports pages beneath a twenty-story fist-cloud of grain dust. And the men themselves, where would they be? the broom? the hammer?

I take a deep breath, my nose swollen with the mai tais, and gather the late sea smell, mixed with the damp odors of Katie, hotel soap, and—faintly—the panda. I step into the surf. These aren't great sandals. I never met a pair of shoes that couldn't be improved by the Pacific Ocean. The waves here are all tamed, and lip in at about four inches. The surf sucks at my heels in the sand. Some lucky tourist is going to look out his balcony and spot a guy in a blue blazer in the ocean and call the police hoping to thwart a suicide. I'd better back out.

I walk back ten feet and then just sit suddenly in the wet sand. The waves can still wash up over my waist and as they do I feel the sure mild tonic of salt on my crotch and it makes me smile. "No, he's just drunk, dear," the tourist is saying to his wife. "Look, he's on an elbow in the surf."

Actually it's a wet journalist, some guy who wanted to his teeth to be a veterinarian, but whose allergies nearly killed him in a routine dissection a month into his first semester, and now he's lost his column and received a bushel of hate mail from the fundamentalists, people not highly evolved enough to know when *i* comes before *e*, letters that hurt regardless of the spelling.

Oh the water feels good sloshing through my trousers. I can tell I'm getting better: the rash will be gone by Wednesday. "Go to plan B," Cracroft had said. It makes me smile. I was already on plan B—or was it C? What a deal. How could I not smile? What would stop me there, half in the ocean, from smiling? Plan B. A person could go through the alphabet. With a little gumption and some love, a person could go through every single letter of the alphabet.

Life in a body is the life for me. That night, coming home from my high school graduation party at Black Rock Beach, Rye and I sang songs. Do you see, we sang. I'm not kidding. We sang this and that and a marathon version of "Graduation Day," by the Lettermen, that went on and on as we made up verses until my street and Rye pulled up to the curb. We crooned the ending until our voices cracked. We sang. I plan on doing it again. Rye pointed at me when I opened the door to get out and said, "Here we go. Good luck, Chief. First night in the real world."

Inside, the house was dark and quiet, everyone in bed. I spent some time sitting in a wedge of light in front of the open fridge making and eating eight or nine rolled ham deals, putting different fillings in the ham each time: pickles, cheese, macaroni. I had failed with Cheryl. I had failed. I felt sad. What I felt was a kind of forlorn that when my mother saw it on my face she would say, "My aren't we a sick chick?" I was a sick chick.

But when I finally went upstairs is when something happened. I'd left my salty shoes on the patio. At the top step, I heard a noise. It was a laugh, my mother's laugh, but I didn't know it was a laugh at that moment. I mean, I thought it might have been a cough or some other noise, but then I went by their room and the door was open and I saw my mother's bare leg in the pale light from the window, the curve of her flank as she rolled, and I went right into my room without stopping and then my heart kicked in and I heard the sound again and I realized it was a kind of laughter. Well, I know all about it now, don't I? This is an easy place from which to know things, a hundred years later a million miles at sea, but then I didn't know and something slammed my chest in such a way that I knew I wasn't going to be able to sleep. I'd graduated from high school, do you see, some sick chick with no sure sense of self, but as I stood at my window for the next four hours until finally some birds began to chitter and the gray light began, a new feeling rose in me. My parents were lovers. Oh sure, oh sure. I know all about it. I knew all about it then, I thought. But the idea killed me. It clobbered me. It filled me with capacity. I didn't have the words for it, nor did I know exactly what it was, but I was certain to my soul that I had the capacity for it. I had grown up in a house with two adults who were lovers. Like wolves or swans, they had mated for life. Years later, I would too. I stood there at the window until my elbows filled with sand and I was heavy with sleep. I could see two neighbor kids walking down the alley. One had a stick and was swinging it against the fences. They were up early, the first sun orange in their hair, and they owned the day. I would give them this one. Through the stunning blue air, I could see the houses of our neighborhood floating away from me. Do you see? That was the first time my heart brimmed. The world was real.